The Family At
Caldicott
Place

Noel Streatfeild

The Family At Caldicott Place

Illustrated by Betty Maxey

 RANDOM HOUSE · NEW YORK

Contents

64338

To the reader of this book

It is usual to think that to be in need of love and a home you must be poor. In England where I live and, I am sure, in the United States too, this is not always true. Athene in this book is a real person. It is very seldom I use a real person in a book but I was so interested in Athene that I had to. She was spending a holiday with people whom I knew. These friends were not rich so everybody had to help around the house. Mostly the children hated helping, for who wants to make beds and wash dishes when there are so many things to do outside? But not Athene. She adored helping, for that was something she had never been asked to do in her life. When you have read this book you will see why.

I am afraid there are Freddies and Sophies around too—children who have plenty of money but no home, no family. I expect you are part of a family. Maybe, in addition to brothers and sisters, you have a family dog like Jelly in this story. Imagine what it would be like to have the money to buy lots of dogs but have no home to bring them to, no place, if it came to that, to keep even a small turtle.

Perhaps now that I have explained about Athene you can understand why, having met her, I felt I must put her in a book and how, because of her, I had to find a home for Freddie and Sophie too.

NOEL STREATFEILD

1.

The Accident

"It is queer," Bill once said, "how you don't notice how nice things are while they are being nice; it's only when they stop being nice that you find out."

Poor Bill, he had every reason to say this and so had Carol and Tim. For, except for the small setbacks which happen to everybody, things had always been so very, very nice until their father's accident.

The Johnstones lived in a new town in a pleasant house with a garden and a garage. Mr. Johnstone was a foreman of a factory in London and drove to and from work every day. He was the best sort of father, always interested in anything his family was doing and he did his best to help. His own hobby was his garden but he was anything but a mean gardener. Most keen gardeners of a not very big but showy little garden say a dog is death to it. The family had—or to be correct, Tim had—a queer little dog. Tim had found him when he was a puppy, lost, miserable and cold. Even though the puppy was small, Tim, who was then only four, had found him heavy to carry and had literally staggered into the house and almost dropped the puppy in the doorway.

"Mum," he had gasped. "Mum. Look what I've found."

"Poor little thing," his mother had said. "We must find out whom he belongs to."

Tim had know she would say that. "He has nothing on his collar. I looked."

By now Bill, who was at that time nine, and Carol who was seven, had joined them.

"I think he's a sort of poodle," Bill had said. "I mean he's got that sort of fur but straight."

Carol had knelt down by the puppy. "His nose isn't quite poodle-ish, more like that dachshund in the pet shop."

4

"Whatever kind of dog he is," their mother had said, "we must ring the police to fetch him."

Six reproachful eyes had looked at her.

"You weren't thinking of taking him to a police station, were you?" Carol had asked in a very shocked voice.

Their mother had weakened. "Not just now, perhaps, but I must let the police know I have him. His poor owner may be waiting for him."

But no owner had been waiting for the little dog that day or any day, so he became a part of the family. He was named Jellicoe because it was by a block of flats called Jellicoe Buildings that Tim had found him, but he was never called Jellicoe—just Jelly.

"Are you sure you want the children to keep Jelly?" Mrs. Johnstone had said to her husband when it was obvious that no one was going to claim the puppy. "He'll ruin your garden."

Mr. Johnstone had laughed. "I'll put fencing everywhere and if Jelly gets through it then I'll make the children replace it. As a matter of fact I'm rather glad Jelly's been forced on us. I should have found it hard to buy a dog, thinking of my flowers, but the children ought to have one. No family is complete without a dog."

Mr. Johnstone, who had made precision tools before he was a foreman, was very neat with his fingers. Anything that his children wanted he was able to make. Angels' wings for the school nativity play. A headdress like a rose when Carol danced in her dancing-class display. In fact so clever was he that over the years when

5

something particularly difficult was wanted for a school
or dancing-class entertainment the teachers would say
to whichever child was involved, "Do you think your
father would help?"

Their father was a great party man. Weeks before
Christmas he always worked out something new and
startling in the way of Christmas decorations with which
to thrill the family and visitors. He always thought out
exciting things too for the family birthdays.

"You pretend you plan things for the children," their
mother would say, "but really it's for yourself. The
trouble is you've never grown up."

Whatever the reason, Mr. Johnstone certainly was a
wonderful planner. Bill's birthday was in August, a time
when the family was away on holiday. Every year,
wherever they went, Mr. Johnstone had what the family
called "Bill's mystery drive" arranged. It was always to
some special place with a superb picnic as part of it,
and it was always the high spot of the holiday.

Carol's birthday was at the end of January and was
kept on the Saturday following it. It was a lunch-out
matinée occasion. But it was no "where shall we eat?"
day. Every moment was worked out by Mr. Johnstone,
and he found thrilling places to eat in, almost always
foreign with strange exotic foods. When the children
were small their mother said she was scared to death in
case one of them should become sick in the theater.

Tim's birthday was the fifth of November and that of
course settled itself. Being Guy Fawkes day it had to
be a bonfire and fireworks party, but what a bonfire

6

and what fireworks! Locally all fireworks were judged by Tim's birthday ones. "They were nearly up to the Tim Johnstone standard" or "They weren't bad but nowhere near the Tim Johnstone style."

It was in August of the year when Bill was going to be thirteen—Carol had been eleven the previous January, Tim would be eight in November and Jelly was believed to be four—that the dreadful thing happened. It was the night before they went away for the summer holidays; they were going to Cornwall that year.

"I'm going to get the car filled up tonight," their father called out. "I don't want to waste time tomorrow because I want to get the back of the journey broken before lunch."

Their mother was packing.

"All right, dear," she answered, her mind on what she was doing.

"Can I go with Dad?" Tim asked.

"No," said his mother. "You don't move until you've laid out on your bed all the toys and things you want to take."

It was one of those accidents which nobody saw. A chauffeur-driven car with an old lady named Lady Paine in the back turned out of a driveway and crashed into Mr. Johnstone's car. The chauffeur was killed and Lady Paine and Mr. Johnstone taken to a hospital unconscious. Without doubt the chauffeur was to blame. Lady Paine's insurance company would pay but not until it was known if Mr. Johnstone was permanently damaged.

He was unconscious for nearly three weeks. Then

slowly he regained consciousness but he came back not like his proper self. It was after he had been conscious for nearly two weeks that Bill went to see him.

"Sister thinks you better see him, Bill," his mother said. "She says he's as well as can be expected but it may be months before he can work again—the doctors are moving him to a psychiatric hospital for treatment." Her voice wobbled she was trying so hard not to cry. "We must make some sort of plan."

"Does Dad know how long he may be ill?" Bill asked.

"The doctors said he was to be told but I don't know if he quite understood. They want him to take an interest in things. But he just won't. Oh, Bill, I'm afraid you're in for a shock, he's so changed."

Bill gave his mother's shoulder an awkward pat. "Don't fuss. He'll be all right in the end."

His mother choked back a sob. "He can't remember what happened, which is natural. But he's so odd. He knows he's been in the hospital for nearly five weeks and he knows we haven't got the insurance money yet, but he seems quite happy to lie there forever. He's not a bit worried about what is to happen to us."

"What do you mean—happen to us?" Bill asked.

His mother hesitated, not wanting to worry him more than she had to. But it was such a relief to have someone to talk to she just burst out with everything.

"The firm is being very good paying Dad as usual, but it can't go on forever. Someday the old lady's insurance company will pay up but that will take time. The doctors say that it may be months before he's back to normal." She again hesitated. "Sometimes I wake in the night scared that he never will be."

Bill felt he was growing up every minute. His father had always been the planner and the arranger for them all. He had never asked Bill for advice—or anybody else if it came to that. Bill supposed Dad really had treated him as a child, which was of course ridiculous when you were almost thirteen. Now he was thirteen and as he talked to his mother, he felt taller and sort of broader in the shoulders.

"I'll visit Dad tomorrow evening. He'll feel different talking to me—you know, not being grown-up and all that."

Bill told Carol and Tim he was going to the hospital, but he didn't tell them anything that his mother had told him. Both of them had, of course, been upset by the accident, particularly Carol who, since it had happened, had cried about anything and was easily cross.

"I know we've all sent flowers and fruit and stuff," Bill said, "but now Dad's getting better can you think up something to send him he might like to do?"

"I could," said Tim, "but I'll save it up for when I visit him."

"That's what I think I'll do," Carol agreed. "If you can go tomorrow perhaps Mum will take us the next visiting day."

"I think there are rules about how many of us he can see," Bill said. "Anyway let me take something from you both tomorrow."

"What sort of thing to do?" Carol asked. "Do you

mean like a jigsaw puzzle?"

Bill shook his head. "No, the hospital will have those. You know the sort of thing he likes doing. It needn't cost much but, of course, should be done up properly seeing what a parcel man he is."

The next evening Bill, with rather a beating heart for he was shy of the big public ward with everyone, he felt, staring at him, turned up at his father's bedside.

His father was propped up in a sitting position and, except that there was a huge scar on his forehead and that he was very pale, he looked far more himself than Bill's mother had led him to expect.

"Hullo, Dad, how're things?"

Very slowly his father turned his head to look at Bill and for a second it seemed as if he did not recognize him. Then he smiled.

"Hullo, old man."

Bill put the parcels and an envelope on the bed.

"This is from Carol, this is from Tim, this is from me and the envelope is from Jelly."

It was then that Bill saw what was frightening his mother. If ever there was a parcel-minded man it had been his father, and that was why the children had done up their parcels in fancy paper. Now his father didn't even give them a glance.

"How kind," he said in a far-away voice and turned his head.

Bill didn't know what to say or do next so he opened Carol's parcel. Carol usually had two-and-sixpence a week pocket money but it never had been enough so her father usually helped out when anything special was wanted. Since the accident the two-and-sixpence had to cover everything including subscriptions, which it never had been expected to cover before. There were therefore signs of poverty about Carol's present. It was packed in last birthday's paper. Inside was an exercise book with lined pages on one side and plain sheets facing it to draw on. On the top of the first page Carol had printed very neatly HOSPITAL DIARY OF FREDER-ICK JOHNSTONE. Bill thought it a wonderful present and it went well with his.

"I say, Dad, look at this." His father held the book which Bill pressed into his hand but he didn't look, so Bill tore open his own present, which was colored pencils.

"And these are just right for drawing in it. You can draw the other patients and the nurses and . . ." He stopped because talking to his father was like talking into space. Miserably he undid Tim's parcel. Tim never had any money saved but he had taken trouble over his present. He had been to the plant shop and persuaded the owner to give him a seed catalogue. He had no birthday paper but he had found an old piece of Christmas paper in which to wrap the catalogue. Bill was full of admiration and sounded it.

"Look what Tim sent you! While you're in bed is just the time to work out what seeds you want to plant. Look at some of these pictures. You know you like looking at catalogues."

His father wouldn't even take hold of the catalogue. "Seeds," he said vaguely. "Please thank Tim."

Bill hardly had the heart to open Jelly's envelope. He knew what was in it for he had bought it himself. It was a get-well card, the sort that usually his father would have thought very funny. It had a picture of a man all bandaged lying in bed, with a fearful-looking wife sitting beside him. Outside it said: "Sorry about your accident." Inside there was a verse about getting well.

"And Jelly sent this card." Bill's voice faded away on "this card" for it was clear his father wasn't listening.

Quite soon the effort of trying to talk without getting an answer was too much for Bill so he got up.

"Good-by, Dad. I'll be in again soon."

It was clear his father didn't care if he came again or not for he just said: "Thanks, old man," and shut his eyes.

At the door of the ward the Sister in charge stopped Bill.

"How did you find your father?"

Bill stared at her with frightened, unhappy eyes. "Awful."

Sister nodded. "I know. But I'm sure he'll pick up when we can move him to the other hospital. Do come again. He may be more interested than you think and anyway if you share the visiting it helps your mother."

Outside the hospital Bill stood pulling himself together. What was he to say to his mother? Suppose his father never got better? What was to happen to them?

2.
Plans

As it turned out Bill did not have to discuss plans with his mother for when he got home he found she had received a telephone call. It was from the manager of the factory where his father worked.

"They want to see me, Bill. The manager was very

kind and said I wasn't to worry, they had a plan to put up to me. I'm to see them tomorrow. How did you think Dad was?"

Bill was going to say "awful," as he had said to the Sister in the hospital, but he bit it back. No good being more depressing than he needed to be. "A bit low, but I suppose he would be after that crack on the head."

"Did he seem interested, I mean in what we're doing and everything?"

Bill struggled between the truth and not sounding too gloomy.

"Well, we'd all sent presents, you know. We talked about them mostly."

His mother had never been to the hospital empty-handed, but never once had the patient seemed to notice anything she brought.

"Talked about them, did he? The Sister must be right and seeing you cheered him up. I wonder if Carol and Tim should see him."

"I'd leave that for a bit—I mean they'd expect him to be as he always was."

His mother saw his point. "All right, we'll stick to just you and me for the time being."

Bill, not wishing to scare Carol and Tim, gave such a good imaginary account of how pleased their father was with their presents that they were upset when the next morning they were told by their mother they couldn't visit him yet.

"It's absolute nonsense!" Tim grumbled to Carol. "I know Dad would like to see me. I wouldn't talk loud."

Carol was equally annoyed but more accepting. "It does seem odd. I mean why can Bill go if we can't? I suppose it's a hospital rule about not too many visitors. You know how fussy they are."

Tim thought Carol was giving in too easily. He took Jelly into the garden and told him all about it. "I didn't tell Carol, but I want to take Dad some of those gladiolas that I've been looking after for him. They're only in bud but they'll come out in water. Dad's awfully proud of them. He took some to work last year to show everybody."

The gladioli, when Tim examined them, had come on a lot. It was now possible to see what color they were going to be. There were two yellow ones, a crimson one, a white one and four mauve ones.

"In two or three days they'll be almost quite out, Jelly," Tim grumbled. "Then I bet Mum picks them and takes them to Dad, which won't be fair because it's me who has watered them and put in sticks so they won't fall over. I don't see why I can't see Dad, it's just hospital silliness. If no one else gets them first I'll just sneak the gladiolas in to him. I know he'll be pleased to see me, and he'd like to see you, but hospitals are terribly fussy about dogs."

That afternoon the children's mother went to London to see the manager of the factory. She came home looking tired but less depressed than she had looked since the accident. She called Bill into the kitchen where she was making a pot of tea.

"I saw Mr. Smith. He was very kind and full of ideas.

Take a deep breath for you're in for a shock. They have, of course, replaced Dad, but it's only temporary. They're holding his job for him for a year."

Bill thought of his father as he had seen him the night before. Well, a year was a long time, and perhaps he'd be well by then. He tried to sound hopeful. "That's good."

"The man who's doing Dad's job at present—his name is Reg Robinson—has been living in one of the firm's flats, but is looking for a larger one. You know Dad and I lived in one of those flats when we were first married. You lived there when you were a baby."

Bill had heard of the flats which they had left when his father was made a foreman. But he couldn't see why his mother was telling him about them now. "Weren't they called Elstob Buildings?" he asked.

"That's right. Funny old-fashioned inconvenient places. The firm built them in the last century. They were considered very up-to-date then. Well, Mr. Smith has had a talk with Reg Robinson and suggested he should rent this house while Dad's ill and we'd take over his flat."

Bill felt as if he'd had a knock in the solar plexus. His mother had said he was to be prepared for a shock, but he'd never thought it would be anything like this.

"But what point would there be in our leaving here?"

"Money. This place takes all my time to keep it clean, but if we moved into Elstob Buildings I could take a job. As you know, I was a secretary when I married your father; well, the firm will find me a secretarial job."

Bill tried to sound sensible. But only the disadvantages came to his mind. "What about our schools?"

"Mr. Smith had thought of that. There's a good comprehensive not too far off where both you and Carol could go."

He and Carol! Bill tried to hide his disgust. It seemed a bit of a come-down to get sent to the same school as Carol. However, he kept what he thought about that to himself. "What about Tim?" he asked.

"There's a junior school almost next door to the Buildings."

Bill thought the whole scheme terrible. "I shouldn't have thought you could type now, it's such ages since you did."

His mother was pleased with the secretarial plan. It would be nice to be earning instead of sitting at home worrying.

"The firm will pay for me to take a refresher course." She hesitated, then said in a firm voice: "I've agreed, Bill. I mean Mr. Smith and the Chairman had thought it all out for us. Of course we'll hate leaving here, but if we stayed I couldn't work—it takes all my time looking after the place. Anyway it's only until Dad's well. We'll be back."

"When are we going?"

"I thought we might wait until Dad is moved to the new hospital. But I called in and saw Sister on my way home. She doesn't think Dad will care that he's not visited. And while I was there I asked whether Carol and Tim should see their father. She said no, it would do him no good, only upset them." She looked at Bill. "I gather she thought seeing him had upset you—you didn't tell me that."

"Well, it's an awful scar." Bill changed the subject. "When do we move to Elstob Buildings?"

"That's to be decided. I've got to go and see the Robinsons' flat, and Mrs. Robinson will come over and see this place. But as we're not moving any furniture, just our personal things, it will be easy."

Bill tried not to show how he felt but he wasn't very successful.

"I suppose we can take our books and things like that. We don't want those Robinsons mucking them about."

His mother understood just how Bill felt, but the facts had to be faced. To her the anxiety about their future had been so wearing that relief helped her over the awfulness of leaving her home. But for Bill it was different. It was tough on Bill facing all the bad news in a lump.

"We must take as little as we can. There are only two quite small bedrooms in Elstob Buildings. Carol will share with me and you will share with Tim . . ."

Share with Tim! Horror piled on horror. Here they each had their own room filled with their own special things. How could he and Tim share? His mother went on relentlessly for she wanted Bill to face all the disadvantages at once.

"There is a very small bathroom and a minute kitchen. And—oh Bill, this is the worst part of it. Jelly can't come. Animals aren't allowed."

That was too much. Jelly wasn't "animals," he was family.

"Jelly can't come!"

"No, but luckily Mr. Robinson will look after him for us. Mr. Smith had remembered we had Jelly. He said Mr. Robinson's two children will be terribly pleased. They've always wanted a dog and been promised one when they had found a house."

Bill felt he had heard enough. "When are you going to tell Carol and Tim?"

His mother poured out her tea. She offered Bill a cup but he shook his head. She was dead tired and she had to go to the hospital for her evening visit.

"When I get home. Oh, Bill, I dread telling them. Carol's been so difficult since the accident, and poor Tim—leaving Jelly behind will break his heart."

Bill looked at her miserably. Leaving Jelly would break all their hearts. It was hard to think of anything cheerful to say.

"Don't fuss," he said in what he could hear sounded like a growl. "We'll get over it."

Directly she got back from the hospital the children's mother broke the news to Carol and Tim. Bill left her to it, making the excuse of "something to do in my room."

"You won't be going to the Secondary Modern in the autumn, Carol, and you are changing schools too, Tim."

"Oh!" said Carol. "Where am I going?"

Tim looked upon school as a necessary evil but he

supposed one was much like another so he didn't say anything.

"It's because we're moving," their mother explained. "I'm renting this house while Dad's ill."

"Renting this house!" It took time for Carol to take this in. "Where are we going?"

"London."

Tim was the only one of the three who had inherited his father's love of a garden. Now he said, "We can't go to London while Dad's ill. Who'll look after the garden?"

"People called Robinson," his mother explained. "They're coming here and we're going into their flat."

Carol had been turning over the strange news while Tim and her mother were talking. Now she let out a sort of mew like a cat whose tail has been trodden on.

"What about my dancing classes? The concert is just before Christmas and I'm to dance a solo, you know I am."

Her mother thought, how stupid of me to have forgotten that charity matinée.

"I daresay something will be arranged. Your classes being Saturdays perhaps you could come back occasionally to rehearse. Anyway there are sure to be good classes in London. I'm certain I can get someone to put you up at the time of the matinée."

Carol didn't answer. Mum never had understood about her dancing classes. If Dad were well he would understand. She had been to the same dancing school since she was five. She had started with baby polkas and pretending to be an elf or a butterfly and then had risen in the world, passing an exam a year to reach the dignified state of wearing a white tunic with a pink belt. Of course she could learn at another school but she wouldn't be in the same position; it would be ages before she was picked to dance a solo at a charity concert.

Mrs. Johnstone plodded on, slipping the pieces of bad news out one at a time.

"There will only be two bedrooms in the London flat. You'll share with me, Carol, and Tim'll share with Bill."

Both Carol and Tim stared at their mother as if wondering if she really meant what she was saying. Except on summer holidays they had always had their own rooms. Tim kept a really magnificent model railway (his father had given it to him piece by piece) permanently set up on his bedroom floor. Then he had a small aquarium of tropical fish. He didn't much care what happened to that, but just now he was making a guy ready for Guy Fawkes day, and his friends came in to help him make it. His bedroom was a working room for himself and his friends. How could he share with Bill, who was always doing homework and had chemistry things all over the place?

Carol just knew that nobody could share a bedroom with her mother. No girl she had ever heard of had done such a thing. What about all those times she and her friends tried standing on their *pointes,* and doing their hair new ways, and playing records? Where would she do those things if she was expected to share a room with Mum?

Tim saw an immediate snag. "Is there going to be a garden in the London flat?"

"I'm afraid not. Flats don't have them. The one we're moving to is a block called Elstob Buildings—flats that belong to Dad's factory. Dad and I lived there when we were first married. Bill was born there."

Tim looked down at Jelly. He was lying on his back fast asleep. "If there's no garden we can't go. Have you thought what it will be like taking Jelly for proper walks with a lead and everything every time he wants to go out?"

His mother did not answer that. "I'm taking a job. I'm going to be a secretary again."

Once more Carol and Tim looked at her as if they thought she didn't know what she was saying. Mum going out to work! Mum away all day! It was nonsense.

"You can't," said Tim. "Who's going to give Jelly his dinner?"

Carol thought of the daily clean clothes ready for her to put on. "Or wash our clothes. And I won't eat school dinners, they're awful."

"And what about Jelly?" said Tim. "Who will be looking after him if you're out and I'm at school?"

Mrs. Johnstone took a deep breath. This was it.

She looked as sorry as she felt.

"Jelly can't come with us. Dogs aren't allowed in Elstob Buildings. The Robinsons will let him stay here."

Some things are too frightful for words. Leaving Jelly behind with the unknown Robinsons was like that. Tim got down on the floor and lay beside Jelly hugging him to him. Carol cried. It was not loud crying, but silent tears that just rolled down her cheeks.

"I know it's awful," Mrs. Johnstone said. "I mind just as much as you."

"You can't," said Tim in a choked voice. "He doesn't sleep on your bed like he does on mine. Usually when I wake his head's on the pillow. Sometimes I'm holding one of his paws."

"He might die of grief," Carol moaned. "Dogs can."

At that moment Bill, wondering if he could help, came back into the sitting room. He heard what Carol said so he knew she and Tim had heard about Jelly.

"Look here, you two. Mum hates all this as much as us. You don't suppose she wants to leave her home or Jelly. But Dad can't earn until he's well and this is the best plan until he is. It's no good making a fuss, it's got to happen."

"If I'm not to make a fuss," said Carol, "then I'm going to bed. It's all awful and I can't pretend it isn't."

Tim got up too. "Come on Jelly. We'll go and look for a cat in the garden. Then we'll go to bed."

"Oh dear!" their mother said to Bill. "I did that badly, I'm afraid."

Bill tried to be helpful. "I wouldn't fuss. We'll all get used to it. It's first hearing everything that's so awful."

"I know. I wish there was some other way, but there just isn't. Mr. Smith had thought of everything."

"I suppose we couldn't get just as cheap a flat in London where Jelly could be with us?"

"You know we couldn't, cheap flats are hard to come by. We wouldn't get into Elstob Buildings if it didn't belong to Dad's firm. Besides, even if we could take Jelly, he couldn't be left alone all day while you children are at school and I'm working."

"They didn't mind changing schools, did they?" Bill asked.

His mother made a face. "No, but I'd forgotten about Carol's dancing class. I'll have to find her another while we're in London. Then there's that concert for the Invalid Children's Aid she was to have danced at. Perhaps I can get her back here for that. I expect someone will put her up. But, as a matter of fact, I must see the head of the dancing school before I leave. Carol's come on a lot and, though she hasn't said so, I think she believes she's good enough to dance as a professional."

Bill was startled. Carol a professional dancer!

"I bet she isn't that good, is she?"

"I haven't an idea, but I must find out, for if there's any thought of such a thing what classes she attends will be very important."

"Did you tell Dad everything last night?"

Bill had seen his father now so his mother looked him squarely in the face.

"I told him. But you've seen him, Bill, so now you know what telling him things is like."

Bill had a lump in his throat. "Yes, now I know."

3.
Gladioli

Carol came down the next morning outwardly calm. It had been a big effort because when she thought of Jelly living with strangers she simply had to cry. But what Bill had said was true. Perhaps Mum was as fond of him as they were and wouldn't leave him behind if there

25

was any way around it.

Her mother gave her a kiss.

"I'm asking for an appointment to see Miss Rome"
—she was the principal—"today. And I'll ask her to
recommend a dancing school in London."

"But what'll I do about rehearsals?"

Mrs. Johnstone was cooking bacon, and she turned the
slices over while she thought about that.

"I suppose, as it's a solo, your new dancing school
could rehearse you. Anyway, let's leave that to Miss
Rome. We'll be guided by her, shall we?"

Privately Carol hoped Miss Rome would say: "Oh,
Mrs. Johnstone, you can't take Carol away from me,
she's the most promising child I ever taught. Couldn't
she stay with me every weekend so she needn't miss a
class?" But what she was thinking did not show on her
face for she was giving Jelly his good-morning kiss. So
all she said was, "O.K."

Tim rushed down to breakfast late and as usual
looking as if he had pulled on his clothes without washing or brushing his hair, which was just what had
happened. There was no sign that he was miserable
about Jelly for he was not. Just before he went to sleep
the night before he had known there must be a way by
which Jelly need not be left behind. He had told Jelly
about it. "I'll get you a home near where we live. I'll
pay for you to sleep there. And every day I'll fetch you
for walks and things. It'll only be sleeping alone. If
my shilling a week isn't enough to pay for where you
sleep I'll get some work. Perhaps I could deliver news-

papers. And the rest of the money I'll spend on your food. Truly, Jelly, you needn't worry. Anyway I'll talk to Dad about it when I take him the gladiolas. He's sure to think of somewhere you can live until we come back here."

Jelly, though he seemed to be listening, was certainly not worrying for soon he had rolled over on his back and, taking up far more than his share of the bed, had gone to sleep. If Jelly was satisfied so was Tim. He went to sleep too.

So when he came down to breakfast it was not Jelly Tim was thinking about, it was the gladioli and seeing his father. If the family was going to move there was no time to waste. Somehow he would have to see Dad today. He was so full of thinking this that he did not take in one word his mother was saying, and so gave the impression that he accepted everything, which was not true at all.

"I know we all hate the idea of moving," the children's mother said as she put the plates of bacon in front of them all, "so there's no point in discussing it. But what we must think about is what, aside from our clothes, we are going to take with us. It's got to be as little as possible because the flats in Elstob Buildings are very small. One little suitcase each—and that means books, games, everything."

Bill gave a quick look at Tim. That cut out his model railway and the aquarium. Was there going to be a row? But Tim just went on eating while he thought: I bet there's another way into the hospital where visitors don't go—people like milkmen.

Mrs. Johnstone too was expecting a row, and she was too grateful when it didn't come to wonder why.

"I suppose the Robinsons will have a television," Carol said.

"Oh, sure to. But I'm seeing the flat so I'll find that out of course, and I'll have a look and see if we can squeeze your gramophone and all your records into the sitting room, Carol."

Carol liked playing her records only when she was alone or had girl friends at tea. Grownups, even Mum, didn't understand what special kinds of music could do to you. She did sort of understand ballet music, but then she generally spoiled it by calling it "pretty." Imagine calling something perfect like the "Swan Lake" music "pretty!" Probably she wouldn't have any girl friends in London, and even if she did she couldn't see them enjoying her records in a small sitting room with all the family there. Anyway, not wanting to bring them was a way to help.

"It's all right, Mum, I can live without them. But I won't have the Robinson's mucking about with my record-player. Will there be any place where we could lock it up?"

Mrs. Johnstone had thought of that. There was a good dry shed where her husband kept his tools and gardening books. There would be room there for just such objects as Carol's gramophone, Tim's not-yet-mentioned model railway, and what was not needed of Bill's chemistry things. There would be some boxes, too; obviously the closets must be cleared but equally obviously they couldn't take all their clothes with them.

"I thought we'd keep Dad's shed. Bless you, Carol. I know your gramophone would have meant a crush in the sitting room. Perhaps you would all start right away deciding what is the maximum you can live without. Remember, if we keep Dad's shed, we could in a real emergency come back for a day and take something out."

After breakfast, Tim, not having listened to a word his mother had said, sketchily tidied his room. Then he went into the garden with Jelly and picked the gladioli. One crimson, two yellow, one white and four mauve. They made a gorgeous bunch. Tim could almost hear his father saying: "Oh, my word, Tim, I'm glad to have those. They've never been better."

After a little snooping around Tim discovered that his mother was going out and Bill and Carol were sorting books and things in their bedrooms.

"I'm sorry you can't come," he apologized to Jelly, "but I'll take you out this afternoon to make up."

It was quite a long walk to the hospital. The ordinary way to go was by bus, but Tim had no money for that so he had to walk. He was very glad when at last he turned in at the gates. But his hopes of finding a special entrance where people like milkmen went in were dashed. There was only one entrance. It was no good hanging about outside so Tim walked up the steps and into the front hall.

It was a large hall with passages leading off in all directions and there were winding stairs and a lift. At the entrance there was a desk with a telephone switch-board behind it. Leaning on the desk was the porter, a man in a white coat.

"Hullo!" he said to Tim. "Who are those for? My, they're fine glads! Did your Dad grow them?"

Tim came up to the desk. "Yes. I'm taking them to him. They'll make him feel better."

The man looked at Tim. "What's your father's name?"

"Johnstone."

The man picked up a list and ran his fingers down it. "Frederick Johnstone?"

"That's right," Tim agreed.

"He's in Sister Thomas's ward. You can't go up there now, son, no visitors until tonight. But you leave the glads with me. I'll see he gets them."

Tim was not going to leave the gladioli with anybody. They were his passport into the ward. He was sure that if Sister Thomas saw the gladioli she would understand. He was just about to explain this when he heard the ringing of an ambulance bell outside and the sound of car doors opening. Then two men in uniform came in carrying a stretcher.

"Accident," said one of the men.

The man with the white coat turned to Tim: "Wait here, son, I shan't be a minute." Then he went away to ring for the lift.

Tim watched him ringing and had an idea. Quick as lightning, clutching his gladioli, he nipped up the stairs.

Tim had no means of knowing where Sister Thomas's

ward was, but now that he was away from the man **at** the desk he found people were helpful. The first person he met was a nurse who beamed at him.

"You'll find Sister Thomas's ward one floor up and through the swing doors."

Then, on the next floor, he met a lady carrying a Hoover.

"Through the swing doors, dear. Ask anybody, they'll find Sister for you."

Then Tim met a young doctor. "Hullo!" he said. "Who might you be?"

Tim tried to sound more certain of himself than he felt. "I'm Tim. My Dad grew these. I'm taking them to him to make him better."

"Who is your Dad?"

"His name is Mr. Frederick Johnstone."

The young doctor knew all about Mr. Johnstone. "I'm afraid you can't see him, but give me the flowers. I'll take them to him."

Tim shook his head. "I must see him. You see, I want to tell him about the gladiolas and about us going to London and what's to happen to our dog. And Dad will want to tell Mr. Robinson, who's coming to our house, how to look after his garden. I mean, Dad will tell me and I'll tell Mr. Robinson."

The doctor knew just how uninterested Tim's father would be in the gladioli or London or anything else. He knew too that it had been decided only the wife and the eldest son were to visit him. He put a hand on Tim's shoulder.

"Leave the flowers with me, old man. I promise I'll

give them to your father and any messages you like."

But Tim wouldn't leave the gladioli. He knew it was silly, but somehow, once he let go of them, he felt he'd never get into the ward. And he had to talk to Dad, he absolutely had to. He moved away from the doctor.

"No, thank you. I'll give them to him myself. Good-by."

Tim meant to walk back the way he had come, and he hoped he could slip out of the hospital without seeing the porter. Once outside and on his own he would have another think. There must be another way to get in, there simply must. But it had been a frustrating morning and the talk with the doctor so disappointing and, in a way, frightening, that he had tears in his eyes. That was why, instead of going downstairs when he was through the swing doors, he went through some more swing doors. And that was how he found himself in the private wing.

The private wing was quite different from the rest of the hospital. It seemed to be all separate rooms with people's names on the doors. There was an open door with a nurse inside sitting at a desk. Tim did not want anyone else asking him to leave the gladioli so he nipped past that room without being seen.

A little farther up the passage a door was ajar and that was how Tim heard the moan. It wasn't exactly the moan of someone who was hurt, more a bored, lonely moan.

"Poor person in there," Tim thought. "I hope Dad

doesn't make noises like that." And he stood on tiptoe to read the name on the door. It said, "Lady Paine."

Lady Paine! "My goodness," Tim told himself, "that was the old lady who was in the motorcar that crashed into poor Dad. But it wasn't her fault, it was the chauffeur's fault, and he was killed. Lady Paine must have been here as long as Dad. I wonder if she'd like someone to talk to." Very quietly Tim pushed the door open wider and stepped into the room.

It was a big sunny room painted white; in the middle was a bed and in the bed, propped up by lots of pillows, was a wrinkled old lady with white hair. What interested Tim was that over her bed was a sort of pulley and this had one of the old lady's legs held in it in a sort of hammock. Tim was so interested in this contraption that he forgot to say good-morning and just walked toward it, staring.

Lady Paine had heard Tim come in and saw what he was looking at. She was short of breath so she spoke in jerks.

"That's to mend my broken leg."

Tim gazed at the pulley. "It's neat. I didn't know you broke your leg. It was Dad's head that was hurt."

"I'm sorry," the old lady panted. "When did that happen?"

Tim thought that a silly question. "On the same day you broke your leg of course. I mean you were both hurt at the same time."

Lady Paine gave a sort of nod as if she understood. "Then your name is Johnstone?"

"That's right. I'm Tim Johnstone."

"But why have you come to see me, Tim Johnstone? And why have you brought me those lovely flowers?"

Tim saw a chair by her bed; he sat down on it. "I didn't really come to see you. I came to see Dad and bring him these—they're from our garden. But they won't let me see him."

As Tim said this he suddenly knew for certain that "they" weren't going to let him see Dad. To his shame, but he couldn't stop once he had started, he began to cry.

Lady Paine let Tim cry. Then, when he had reached the hiccuping, dripping stage, she pointed to a box of paper handkerchiefs on the bed table which was in front of her.

"You'd better use some of those."

Tim took two or three and after much nose-blowing and wiping felt better.

"Carol and me," he explained, "hadn't seen Dad since the accident but I always thought we could if we wanted to. Then yesterday Mum said we couldn't visit him yet. And now we're going to London and it may be ages before I see him. I've such lots to ask him. And I don't care what they say, I know he'd like to see me."

"Why are you going to London?" Lady Paine asked.

"Our house here is being rented while Dad's ill. People called Robinson are going to live in our house and we're moving into their flat, which is in a place called Elstob Buildings. It's only got two bedrooms, but the worst thing is Jelly can't come."

"And who is Jelly?"

"Our dog—well, mine sort of, because I found him. But he's family. He's not exactly any kind of dog because most of him is poodle without the proper curls, and his nose and ears are like a dachshund's. He's my best friend."

"What will happen to him while you are in London?"

Tim somehow felt he could trust Lady Paine. "They think he's going to stay with the Robinsons but of course he can't. He'd die away from us. So I'm going to find a place he can sleep and then, except for school, he can be with me all day and I'll feed him."

Lady Paine had closed her eyes. She took so long a time answering that Tim thought she was asleep, but she wasn't. At last she panted: "I think I'd give the Robinsons a chance. I have had several dogs in my life—not now, my old pug died two years ago. But it has been my experience that if I was away the kindest thing was to arrange for my dog to stay at home. Dogs like places they are used to."

"But I'd never see him," Tim protested.

"London isn't far. I expect you could visit him sometimes, couldn't you?"

Tim much preferred his own plan for Jelly. But he knew it might be necessary for Jelly to start by living with the Robinsons.

"If only I knew how long Dad would be ill," he said. "Nothing would be so bad if I knew that."

Lady Paine nodded. "I know, Tim. Nothing would be so bad if we knew that. You must go now for I am too tired to talk any more. If you come back to see Jelly will you come to see me?"

Tim nodded. "Of course. I hope your leg is well soon."

"And if I were you I'd write a nice message to go with those flowers and tell the porter to take them up to your father."

Tim looked around the bare room. There were no flowers. It seemed to him it must be sad to be alone with a broken leg and no flowers. He laid the gladioli on the bed table.

"You have them. Dad doesn't know they're out so he won't miss them." Then he tiptoed out of the room.

"Hullo, young fellow my lad," said the porter. "Where did you get to? Did Sister let you see your Dad?"

"No."

The porter made a man-to-man face. "I was afraid she wouldn't. Sticklers for rules they are. But you left the glads, and he'll enjoy them."

Tim saw no need to answer that.

"Good-by," he said politely. "I must go or I'll be late for dinner."

4.
Half-term Holiday

Some things are so awful it's like having influenza or measles; they have to be endured but not remembered. The move to Elstob Buildings was like that. Everybody meant to try hard and not to grumble but the family were so on top of each other in the tiny flat it was very difficult to stick to good intentions. Each of the Johnstones found certain conditions intolerable.

In his new school Bill was placed in a class that in some subjects was ahead of the class in his old school. This meant he had to work extra hard to catch up. So each day, when he came home loaded with homework, it was more than he could bear when he found Tim playing with a new friend in their tiny bedroom. Bill tried desperately hard to be fair, but when a fairly polite "Could you two play somewhere else?" was not immediately answered there were days when he snapped, "I said, get out." Then, of course, there was a row, which made Bill feel he had been a beast and this prevented him from working well.

Carol loathed sharing a room with her mother even more than she had expected she would. If only, she thought miserably, Mum would try less hard. There was so little closet and drawer space, and her mother would try to take less than her share. Carol thought this maddening for it made her feel guilty, as if she had grumbled about being squashed, which she hadn't. And how she wished Mum would say, "Isn't sharing awful for both of us?" instead of saying, as she often did, "I find sharing with you rather fun, darling. It means I see more of you and hear everything you are doing." There wasn't an answer to a thing like that.

Then, too, Carol was unhappy about her new dancing class. Her mother had come back from seeing Miss Rome simply saying that Miss Rome knew of a very good dancing school in London and was writing to the head of it.

The new school was very good, Carol knew that, but it was not friendly in the way her old school had been. In fact, Carol had a feeling that the teachers rather despised her, for they were always picking on her for small faults. It never struck her that Miss Rome had asked them to take extra trouble as there was a possibility Carol was outstanding.

Tim, in spite of what Lady Paine had said, had not accepted life without Jelly. In fact he was giving all his mind to finding him a home. The best thing for Jelly, he had decided, would be to live with one of Tim's schoolmates who would like to share Jelly with him. That was why he was always bringing boys home to play. He tried a new one out each day, always working around to finding out if dogs were allowed, praying someone would say "yes." Tim was appalled to discover that in London there seemed to be no flat where dogs were allowed and no boy he talked to knew of a place where a dog could be boarded. But he made a lot of friends who longed to have a dog and liked hearing about Jelly.

The children's mother was always over-tired. All week she worked and on Sundays she traveled by bus to the psychiatric hospital to which the children's father had been moved. At home she struggled to be the same gay Mum the children had always known. She tried to cook extra nice suppers because they all had to have school dinners. She tried not to be cross when she found that Tim had messed up the kitchen making toast for himself and a friend. She tried, when she came home from work, to be interested in what the children had been doing. But it was acting, not real, and the children could feel it. She had found going back to work after fourteen years of not working very hard. At the refresher course she had got by, but now that she worked in the office of the factory she was not doing so well. The director she was secretary to, knowing who she was, tried to be patient but she could hear his patience running out when for the fourth time she said, "I'm sorry I missed that. Could you dictate a bit slower?" She knew it was only a matter of time before she would be down-graded to the typing pool.

Because each of the family was miserable in a different way and never discussed what was making them miserable, living squashed together in Elstob Buildings was like living on a mine. The question was when would the explosion come and who would start it off?

When the explosion came it happened because of a series of events. It was just before the half-term holiday. Monday Carol was to go to her old dancing class to be rehearsed by Miss Rome in her dance for the charity concert. Tim was to travel with her to have lunch with the Robinsons so that he could see Jelly. Bill was looking forward to Monday because he would have the flat to himself. There was nothing special he wanted to do but it would be the first time since they had lived in the place that he could spread himself.

Then everything went wrong. It started when the mail arrived on Saturday morning. There were two letters, one for Carol and a typed one for Mrs. Johnstone.

She did not open her letter, being sure she knew what was in it. The night before, the manager had seen her. He had tried to be kind.

"Look, Mrs. Johnstone, for the time being I'm moving you into the typing pool. You've done very well but you need a bit more practice to get your speed up. Now, don't fret about this. Your money will be the same and perhaps later on we can fix you up with one of the other directors."

Don't fret indeed! Mrs. Johnstone had minded dreadfully. The girls in the typing pool were all young, straight from school in fact. What a fool she would look working with them! The fact that her money was unchanged made things worse because it was more than was paid in the typing pool and so she couldn't take pride in earning it. Like her children, she had got into the habit of keeping unhappy things to herself so she had not told them what had happened. Instead, when Carol was asleep, she had let herself go and really cried for the first time since the car accident. As a result she had woken up tired and with a headache. "And I won't open this letter," she thought now, "for I'm sure it's merely an official notification of what I was told yesterday. And I'm not in the mood to read it." Nor was she in the mood to comfort Carol, who suddenly burst into tears.

"Whatever is the matter?" Mrs. Johnstone asked.

Carol pushed her letter across to her mother.

"Read that."

"Carol dear,

I do hope you won't be disappointed but on the advice of the teachers at your new dancing school I am cutting out your solo at the concert here. It is a great disappointment to me not to have you but your teachers are working hard, as you know, on a posture fault and on your arms and they feel that if you work for this concert without constant supervision, these faults may grow worse instead of disappearing. Do not be too upset, Carol dear. I can promise you it's a compliment they are taking such an interest in you.

Your affectionate teacher,
Helen Rome."

"It's the last straw that's broken this camel's back," Carol sobbed. "I could bear everything because of that concert and now it's not going to happen."

It was at that moment that the telegram arrived—there was no telephone in the flat. It was from the Robinsons:

CHILDREN HAVE MEASLES MUST PUT TIM OFF MONDAY.

Tim was outraged. "Why should I be put off? I don't mind them having measles. Jelly hasn't got measles and it's him I'm going to see."

His mother could have screamed but she managed to say: "Poor Mrs. Robinson. With the children to nurse she can't give you lunch."

"Anyway you couldn't go," Carol sobbed, "now that I'm not going."

Tim was furious. "I can go alone. I can take sandwiches and Jelly's dinner, can't I? I only want to take Jelly for a walk. I never did want to see the Robinsons."

His mother tried to be patient. "You know you can't go alone so don't talk rubbish." Then she turned back to Carol. "Don't cry, Carol. I see Miss Rome says it's a compliment."

"She can keep her compliments," sobbed Carol. "I was to wear a pink tutu and I've never worn a tutu. Miss Rome was borrowing it for me."

Suddenly all Bill's loathing of being squashed into a small flat boiled to the surface. It was ghastly enough when everybody behaved reasonably but with Carol mewing about pink tutus and Tim going on about Jelly, life was unbearable.

"Shut up, all of you! Shut up!" he shouted.

That was the last straw for his mother. Bill, the person she trusted not to flap, starting to shout. She got up and held out her letter.

"I'm sorry for all your disappointments but you aren't the only ones. You know I've been a private secretary —well, I've been down-graded. This letter is, I imagine, to confirm what I was told yesterday." She slit open the envelope and pulled out a crisp, rich-looking sheet of notepaper. It was headed, "Rawson, Pulson and Crome. Solicitors." She read it twice. Then she looked at Tim.

"When did you meet Lady Paine?"

Tim was interested in nothing but how to get Jelly out for a walk on Monday. "In the hospital. Why?"

"She's dead," his mother said. "The accident killed her, poor old lady."

Carol was still sniffing. "Why should Tim have known her?" she asked.

Mrs. Johnstone stared back at the letter. "This is not about me, it's from Lady Paine's solicitors. She's left you a house, Tim."

Of course there had to be a celebration—it isn't every day someone inherits a house. And, since it was the one way of celebrating that Tim wanted, his mother went out to a telephone box and rang up Mrs. Robinson. She came back smiling.

"Get ready, all of you. The Robinson children aren't too ill, but I think Mrs. Robinson has enough to do and was very glad to hear we'll take Jelly for a walk. We'll have lunch at that new restaurant in High Street and fetch Jelly afterwards."

It felt queer to be going as visitors to the place where they had lived. But the family had a splendid lunch of chicken and fruit salad and ice cream, after which they set off in good spirits to fetch Jelly.

Mrs. Johnstone went to the front door. The children looked over the gate, peering around to see if there was anything wrong with their place. There wasn't. The garden looked tidy and brushed up, and the geraniums had been lifted and put away for the winter just as their father had always done. Then, before they could look

44

any more, Jelly came out of the house barking. If ever barks said, "It's my family back. It's my family back. My own family. They haven't left me. I knew they wouldn't," Jelly's did.

"Angel, angel Jelly," said Carol.

Bill tried to hold him. "Stand still so we can see how you look."

Tim couldn't say anything, he was so pleased to see Jelly again.

They took Jelly to the local park where he could run about without a lead.

"I don't doubt he's missed us," said the children's mother, "but he has not pined—in fact I think he's put on weight."

"Probably he doesn't get enough walks," Bill suggested.

Mrs. Johnstone laughed. "It's no good trying to pick holes in the way the Robinsons look after him. Mrs. Robinson says the children adore him—he sleeps on one of their beds. They stick exactly to the diet sheet we gave them. Wet or fine he has two good walks a day, he's brushed every morning and goes to the dog shop to be cut once a month."

"I must say he looks pretty good," Carol agreed.

But Tim said nothing. It was, of course, a relief to see Jelly looking so well but really he would have preferred his appearance to show how badly he'd missed them. It would be terrible if he grew to love the Robinsons more than he loved them. When for a moment he was alone with Jelly he whispered in his ear: "You aren't

45

belonging to those Robinsons. You belong to us and somehow you're coming to live with us. I promise. I absolutely promise."

Jelly gave him a loving look and licked his face.

The awful part of the day was taking Jelly home. He might be happy with his new family but it was clear he felt that his own family was back for good.

"You take him to the front door, Tim," said Mrs. Johnstone. "And remember to thank Mrs. Robinson for looking after him so beautifully."

Tim led Jelly to the front door. It seemed idiotic to ring the bell of his own home but of course he had to, and as he rang, it seemed as if Jelly suddenly realized that his family was once more abandoning him. Down fell his tail, and as he looked up at Tim there seemed to be tears in his eyes. Tim was very nearly crying himself.

"It'll be all right, Jelly. I absolutely promise."

It was Mr. Robinson who opened the door. "Hullo!" he said. "Brought the dog back? Hope you think he's looking O.K."

Tim could only manage a rather choked whisper. "Yes, thank you. Good-by." Then he put the lead in Mr. Robinson's hand and without another look at Jelly turned and ran to the gate.

All the family felt miserable about leaving Jelly but it was clear from Tim's face that he felt worse than any of them. Nothing could cure the hurt but perhaps, his mother thought, food would comfort.

"Now where shall we have tea?" she said. "I feel in

46

the mood for crumpets with a lot of butter."

On Monday Mrs. Johnstone stayed away from work.

"Partly because it's your half-term," she told them, "partly because I want to see the lawyers about Tim's house. But mostly it puts off the typing pool for another day. I'll ring up the office and explain."

After breakfast she went out and telephoned both to the office and the lawyers. She came home smiling.

"Everything's all right. I've an appointment with the solicitors at three. They want you to come too, Tim. Now, if I make out a list, Carol, will you and Tim do the shopping? I want to cook a special lunch to take away the taste of all those school dinners you're always grumbling about."

But when Carol and Tim had gone off with the shopping bag his mother said to Bill: "I got rid of them because I want to talk to you. I want your advice. When I was at the new hospital yesterday I saw the doctor who looks after Dad. I don't think they are going to keep him much longer."

Bill gave a dismayed whistle. "Goodness! Whatever shall we do? There's no room here."

They were in the kitchen. His mother sat down at the table. "There's no thought of that. I didn't understand all the doctor said but it seems that what Dad needs now is somewhere quiet where he can be on his own a lot."

"Can't he go to a convalescent place?"

"He could, and if we can't think of something better that's where they will send him. The doctor thought we

47

might have relations who lived in the country or by the sea."

Bill thought about their relations. Mum's parents lived in Exeter in a small flat on a noisy council estate. Dad's parents were dead. There was an uncle on Mum's side but he had five children and anyway he lived in Bradford. Dad had a sister but she was a school teacher living in the middle of Belfast. It was Dad and Mum who had been the well-off part of the family, with whom other members came to stay.

"I suppose you told the doctor how we're fixed?" Bill asked.

His mother nodded. "Yes. But he still wished we could think of something. He said Dad would get well much quicker if we could. A convalescent home isn't what he needs."

"How about Tim's house?" Bill suggested. "Perhaps that's in the country."

"That's what I wanted to talk to you about. Wherever Tim's house is it will have to be sold, of course, and the money invested for Tim. But there will be the insurance money coming. Do you think that Tim ought to be told what the doctor wants? I mean that if his house is sold quickly he could lend Dad the money to get away somewhere."

Bill couldn't see what his mother was fussing about. "Of course tell him. Tim would be furious if he found he was in the money and hadn't been given the chance to lend it to Dad."

His mother got up. "What a comfort you are, Bill."

Bill looked sheepish. "I'm sorry I shouted at everybody on Saturday but it is pretty horrible here, isn't it?"

His mother made a face. "Revolting."

After lunch Tim and his mother set out for the solicitors' offices. On the bus his mother told Tim about his father.

"I think we could find a place he'd like where he can potter in a garden and perhaps take up fishing—the doctor was very keen he should fish. If the solicitors can get money for your house would you like to lend it to Dad until we get the insurance money?"

Tim could not imagine himself owning a house. It was what the letter said but it didn't sound true. He thought that when they got to the solicitors' he would hear it was all a mistake. But naturally he wanted to help Dad if Mum knew how he could.

"Of course I would."

His mother looked at him expecting him to ask questions. But Tim had room in his mind for only one worry. Jelly. He couldn't get over the tears he thought he had seen in Jelly's eyes. Besides, he had promised.

Tim and his mother were shown into a large office. A gray-haired gentleman got up from his desk as they came in.

"I am Mr. Crome senior. How do you do, Mrs. Johnstone? And how do you do, Timothy?"

Tim liked the look of Mr. Crome senior. "I'm just called Tim."

Mr. Crome senior asked them to sit down. Then from

a drawer he took a large parchment with green tape around it.

"This is the last Will and Testament of the late Lady Paine. She told me of your visit to her in the hospital, Tim, and how you had given her some flowers."

"Gladiolas," said Tim. "They were for Dad really but I wasn't allowed to see him."

His mother gazed at Tim as if he were a stranger. "I never heard about you visiting Lady Paine. You never told me."

Tim dismissed that. "There was nothing to tell."

"Anyway," Mr. Crome senior went on, "your visit pleased her very much. Immediately afterwards she made a codicil to her Will—a codicil is rather like adding a P.S. to a letter. In the codicil she said"—he read from the Will—" 'I leave to Timothy Johnstone my property in Sussex and the contents. I leave this to him unconditionally either to live in or to sell. The decision to be his alone.' " Mr. Crome senior laid down the Will and opened a drawer and took out a sheet of paper. "This is a description of your property, Tim. The house is called Caldicott Place. It is a Georgian house standing in twenty acres of land, part of which is wooded. There is also a stream with, so I believe, excellent trout fishing. In the house there is a big entrance hall, four reception rooms—that means dining rooms, drawing rooms and so on. Six principal bedrooms, four smaller bedrooms, staff accommodation, and there are stables which can be used as a garage."

Tim's mother's face had a glazed look. "It's a palace," she said.

Mr. Crome senior shook his head. "A very tumble-down palace, I'm afraid. Lady Paine did see that the roof was repaired and a woman came in regularly to air the place and keep an eye on the furniture, but the grounds have been completely neglected and the house is very old-fashioned. Only two bathrooms and no central heating."

"It sounds as though it will be difficult to sell," Tim's mother said.

Mr. Crome senior nodded. "I fear so. It would need an enormous sum spent on it to make the house comfortable. And today few people want to buy houses that size. Its best chance would be as a country club or small hotel but I fear we are very unlikely to find a client prepared to invest the money needed to make Caldicott Place habitable."

"Then what do you suggest?" Tim's mother asked.

"I think it likely the property could be sold as a building site. I would not suggest that Tim should wait for his money but that we should find a buyer immediately who specializes in purchasing property for development."

Tim's mother had been having a horrid mental vision of Tim's property lying idle while she, out of the little money she had, paid a woman to open windows and let herself in for other expenses as well. So she let out an enormous sigh of relief.

"Oh, thank goodness! I was afraid you meant no one would buy it. Please find someone who specializes in buying properties to develop as quickly as you can."

Tim had not understood one quarter of this. But he

had understood perfectly what Lady Paine had said in her Will. He had a house called Caldicott Place. It had fishing for Dad and was perfect for Jelly. He listened to the words "buy" and "sell" tossed across Mr. Crome senior's desk, but Lady Paine had written that only he was to decide whether he would live in his house or whether he would sell it. Mum and Mr. Crome senior seemed to have forgotten this. Lady Paine knew about Elstob Buildings and Jelly having to stay with the Robinsons because he had told her. That was why she had given him a house. Mum and Mr. Crome senior just didn't understand. Tim stood up and leaned across Mr. Crome senior's desk.

"I'm not going to sell my house, Mr. Crome senior," he said firmly. "It's got fishing for Dad, which the doctor said he was to have, and it's got tons of room for Jelly. So I'm going to live there."

5.
Tim's House

Mr. Crome senior and Mrs. Johnstone tried to make Tim see that he couldn't live in Caldicott Place. But what they said just passed him by. He had a house where Dad could fish and Jelly could live. What was there to argue about? Then Mr. Crome senior had a thought.

"In a few minutes my secretary will bring in tea. Tea in this office is only a cup of tea and a biscuit. I'm sure you won't think much of that, Tim. My grandson, who has just joined the firm, probably enjoys a good tea as much as you do. I suggest he takes you out while I look after your mother." Then, without waiting for Tim to answer, he spoke on the telephone.

"Miss Sawyer, will you please ask Mr. James to come to my office, and we shall be two for tea."

Mr. James Crome looked youngish, even to Tim who thought all grownups were old. He shook hands with Tim's mother and grinned at Tim.

"You wanted me, Grandfather?"

"Yes. You knew about Lady Paine's Will. This is Tim who has inherited Caldicott Place. His mother and I were advising that the property should be sold for development but Tim insists he wishes to live there. I suggest you take him to some place where they serve a good tea and you could discuss the matter together."

Mr. James Crome knew a splendid place for tea, and when the waitress had left them at a table crowded with food, and Coca Cola to drink, he asked Tim about Caldicott Place.

"So you want to live on your property, do you?"

Tim liked James Crome. He felt he was a man who would understand about dogs.

"It's Jelly," he explained. "He's my dog though really he's family. We had to move to Elstob Buildings when Dad had his accident because our own house was too big for Mum to look after and earn money typing. Well, you can't have dogs in Elstob Buildings so Jelly has stayed with the Robinsons, who are living in our house. And last Saturday we went home and took him out. Everybody said he looked well and fatter but I took him back to Mr. Robinson. Did you know dogs could cry real tears? Well, Jelly did. So I promised him somehow I'd have a home for him and now I have one. I thought perhaps we could move there next week."

James Crome had a spaniel called Lady. Year after year he refused invitations to go abroad for his holiday because Lady couldn't come, so he understood exactly how Tim felt about Jelly.

"But if my grandfather could sell Caldicott Place you could go back to your own home. I mean, there wouldn't be any need for your mother to work if that happened. You'll be in the money."

Tim took a second slice of well-buttered toast with gentleman's relish—a delicacy new to him.

"It's Dad. I don't know exactly why but part of his getting well is to fish. Mum said so. Our house is in a town so you can't fish there. So when Mr. Crome senior said you could catch trout in the garden of my house that was a double reason."

James Crome drank some Coca Cola while he thought of the best way to explain.

"I've seen Caldicott Place. My grandfather sent me down to make some arrangements after Lady Paine died. It's no end of a big place. More like a club than a home. I don't see how your mother could look after it. And you can't call the land around it a garden—it's what's known as an estate."

For a moment Tim stopped eating.

"I didn't think of us living in all of it. All we need is a bedroom each and somewhere to eat. The kitchen could do for that. And we can just have a little garden and leave the rest alone. People can come for holidays —you can if you like."

James Crome stopped eating. "Tim," he said, "something is stirring in the gray matter. An idea is being born."

Back in the office over cups of tea Tim's mother was telling Mr. Crome senior all about her husband. Mr. Crome senior was a good listener. He made her tell him every single thing the doctors had said and he never interrupted once. When she had told him all she knew he said:

"Pity, really, that young Tim can't get his wish and live in Caldicott Place. It would be perfect for your husband. He could even be alone, if that's what the doctors advise, for there's a lodge that could be made habitable, and as Tim reminded us there is the trout stream."

Tim's mother sighed. "I know. But how could I look after a place that size?"

Mr. Crome senior smiled. "Of course you couldn't. I meant if things were different I would be glad if Tim could have his wish. But as things are we'll have to talk young Tim into selling—in fact I hope my grandson has already done so. However, that will mean that as soon as it can be arranged you can stop working and go back to your own home, so Tim will have his dog with him again."

It was as he said this that Tim and James Crome burst into the room—and burst is the proper word—something that had never happened before in Rawson, Pulson and Crome's.

"Mum," said Tim. "Jim—he told me I could call him that—he's had a simply marvelous idea."

James Crome felt his grandfather thought his entrance had not been sufficiently dignified. He straightened his tie.

"I was telling Tim that really Caldicott Place was big enough for a club and something Tim said gave me the tip. Those wards of the firm's—wouldn't Caldicott Place be just the ticket if Mrs. Johnstone would agree? Kids that age aren't fussy so it wouldn't mean much doing up of the house."

Mr. Crome senior thought and as he thought a rather pleased look came over his face.

"It is an idea. It certainly is an idea." He turned to Tim's mother. "Could you manage to go down and look at Caldicott Place, Mrs. Johnstone, and of course you too, Tim?"

"I suppose so," Tim's mother agreed. "When?"

"The sooner the better. Tomorrow if you could manage it."

"I could drive you," Mr. James Crome offered. "Got a station wagon. Take the whole family and pick up Jelly on the way."

"Oh, Mum, do let's go," Tim begged.

"But why should I look at it?" Tim's mother asked.

Mr. Crome senior's eyes twinkled. "My grandson is suggesting enlarging your family. The country has many children in it, Mrs. Johnstone, who, though they are well endowed with money, have nothing else. Three such children are wards of this firm. They are at boarding schools at the moment, but one at least must be moved and none of them has anywhere definite to go for Christmas. What they need, Mrs. Johnstone, is a mother and a home."

Tim's mother stared at Mr. Crome senior while what he had said took possession of her mind. Then she got up. She turned to James Crome.

"Please take us to see Tim's house tomorrow." Then she looked at Mr. Crome senior. "I'm not saying anything yet. But it is an idea. It certainly is an idea."

In a burst of confidence Mrs. Johnstone telephoned the factory to say she was giving up work. The next day the family, together with Jelly and Jim's Lady, set off in the station wagon for Sussex. It was a lovely day. There was a pale blue sky, a little wind was blowing which sent dead leaves twisting and turning off the trees. The hedges were misty with traveler's joy, through which glistened the bright red of rose hips and the darker red of the haws. Tim's house was close to the Sussex downs.

"Not too far from Eastbourne or Brighton," Jim—as they had all been told to call him—told the family, "but for a populated county The Place is very isolated, though there is a village with a general shop where I imagine you can buy most things."

Living in a suburban town, and spending their holidays in seaside resorts, the children had never known real country or seen a house anything like Tim's. As Jim drove his station wagon through wrought iron gates and up a long driveway to an open space by the front door, the family, who had chattered all the way down from London, were silent. None of them, not even the children's mother, noticed the weeds in the driveway or that the house looked unlived in and uncared for. What they saw was the sort of place they imagined the royal family living in at Sandringham, and not one of them pretended not to be impressed.

"Gosh!" said Bill.

"It's the Sleeping Princess's palace," Carol whispered.

"Look." Tim spoke to Jelly. "You can run and run forever and you'll never need a lead."

"My dear Jim!" Mrs. Johnstone gasped. "Your grandfather never said it would be like this."

Jim had been thinking a lot about his plan for Caldicott Place and talking it over with his grandfather. The last thing he wanted was that Mrs. Johnstone should be put off before she had even seen the house.

"Come and look at the inside. My grandfather telegraphed Mrs. Pennywell—she's the one who keeps an eye on the place—to light a fire so we could have our picnic by it." He held out a key. "Come on, Tim, unlock your front door."

Mrs. Pennywell had heard them arrive and hurried through from the back to meet them. She was a cheerful red-cheeked woman wearing rubber boots, a felt hat and an overcoat. Over her coat she wore a blue-checked apron.

"Sort of outdoors and indoors," Carol said afterward.

"Ah, there you are!" said Mrs. Pennywell. "Seems funny-like having people coming in at the front door. I've lit the fire in what was the housekeeper's room— at least that's what it's called in the plan. It's a small room so it heats up easy."

The hall was so big it was like going into a church. Mrs. Pennywell was used to the place and consequently unimpressed. She led the way across the hall and through a door covered in green baize.

"There's no gas or electricity turned on, of course, so I've put a kettle on the fire." She smiled at Mrs. Johnstone. "I thought you'd want a cup of tea."

After a splendid picnic by the fire Mrs. Johnstone said: "I'm going to get Mrs. Pennywell to show me the house. You children go around with Jim."

Mrs. Pennywell, having been told of the plan for using the house, was encouraging.

"I don't see you will need to open up all these big rooms," she said as she led the way through a vast dining room to a vaster drawing room, and on to a huge study-cum-library and a second rather smaller drawing room. "There's not really enough furnishings for the one room. If it was me I'd turn this smaller drawing room into a sitting room and I'd make that little room where you had your picnic into a dining room."

Mrs. Johnstone drew her coat around her. "How could I heat the place? It's so cold."

"Fires," said Mrs. Pennywell. "Any amount of wood for free on the property."

Mrs. Johnstone looked out of the window at what to her seemed like a public park and tried to imagine free wood.

"But who'd cut it up and how would I get it to the house?"

"My son-in-law Sam could help at that and no doubt your boys would lend a hand. My son-in-law works for the Council but between times he can turn his hand to most things."

Upstairs Mrs. Pennywell led the way to a bathroom. "You'll need to put in heaters for the bath water, but it won't be too big a job for there's electricity laid on all over the house. Lady Paine's father had it done. Lady Paine was brought up here when she was a child."

Out of the bathroom and walking along a vast passage to the principal bedrooms Mrs. Johnstone said: "Even if we open up only a few rooms there's a terrible lot to keep clean."

"If the children who are coming can pay well, as you say they can, you won't have too much trouble about that. I can come every day and, if pressed, my daughter —her that's married to Sam—could lend a hand."

They were in what was designated in the description of the house as a master bedroom. There was a bed in it covered by a dust sheet. Mrs. Johnstone sank down on it.

"I'm not used to a place like this, Mrs. Pennywell. We've got a lovely home but you could get the whole

61

of it in the entrance hall here. I'm terrified of taking this place on and I wouldn't consider it except for my husband. He's been in a bad car smash, and the doctors want him to be in a place where he can be a lot on his own and where he can fish."

"Lovely fishing there is," said Mrs. Pennywell. Then she laughed. "There's many hereabouts could tell you about that. Bad news for the fishers it will be if you come to live here. You couldn't call them poachers, not really. I mean—all those fish doing nothing—well, you can't blame anyone, can you?"

The children's mother had never fished and was not interested in it. "I'm not the sort of person to live in a place like this. I'm just a suburban housewife, and that's what I like being."

Mrs. Pennywell gave Mrs. Johnstone a smile that was like a friendly pat. "You've had a bad time I can see. Don't be afraid of the house, dear. It's a nice old place when you're used to it. Then think of us. We've been scared around here that it would be sold for a building site. It would spoil the countryside, that would."

Mrs. Johnstone was surprised. "Would it! I should have thought you'd love it. I mean, it would bring more life to the neighborhood and better shops and . . ."

Mrs. Pennywell shook her head. "We don't want more of that here. We're farming folk hereabouts, sheep mostly but a bit of arable, and we like things the way they are."

Mrs. Johnstone hid her amazement. To her the community where her home was seemed absolutely perfect. Nice neighbors all with the same sort of income. A good shopping center. Good schools. And plenty going on. Could anybody really like living miles from anywhere? All the same, if she did not understand her she liked Mrs. Pennywell and talking to her cheered her up.

"Let's have a look at the smaller bedrooms," she said. "If we decide to come here—and it's a very big if— they'll be the ones we'll use."

6.
The Move

For many days the move to Caldicott Place hung in
the balance, for Mrs. Johnstone was scared to take it
on and said so. It was a talk with the doctor at the
hospital which convinced her that she ought at least
to try the experiment.

"It's splendid!" the doctor said. "Nothing could be better. Just what I would have chosen for your husband's convalescence. A lodge where he can live entirely on his own is exactly what he needs."

"Can he come for Christmas?" Mrs. Johnstone asked. "He's always made such a thing of Christmas."

The doctor shook his head. "He's not well enough to take part in festivities this year. But he should be fit to live on his own sometime in January."

Mrs. Johnstone was disappointed, but still, January was not far off. "That will give me time to get the lodge ready for him."

"Don't do too much getting ready. Of course see that it's warm and all that, but a large part of the cure will be his doing things for himself. I understand he's a keen gardener. Well, if he feels like it, let him garden."

"And fish," Mrs. Johnstone reminded him. "You said he was to fish."

The doctor laughed. "Not in January. It's a closed season for trout, and we don't want him being brought up before a magistrate. But he can fish in March. Wonderful for him. I would like to come and see him in April and bring a rod with me. Imagine a private trout stream!"

Well, of course that settled things. Mr. Crome senior was delighted.

"And don't worry about money," he told Mrs. Johnstone. "You have the insurance money coming so this firm can safely advance you all that is needed. And then there is the money from the wards of the firm."

It was Mr. Crome senior's saying that which made Mrs. Johnstone think of the children who were coming.

"Do you know, in all the fuss about the house and worrying about my husband, I haven't thought about the children. Tell me about them."

They were in Mr. Crome senior's office. Usually when he discussed anything he took papers out of a drawer and made notes on them, but when talking about the three children who were wards of the firm he evidently needed no aid to his memory.

"Freddie Tove is Lord Burton's heir. His mother died when he was born. His father got into trouble but before the law caught up with him he skipped off to Australia. He's married again and doing well and has quite a family, I believe. The grandfather brought the boy up but he died four years ago. He never forgave his son so he settled all his money on Freddie and made us his guardian. He is at a preparatory school and goes to Eton next autumn. He is twelve."

Mrs. Johnstone was horrified. "What do we call him?"

"Freddie, of course. As the son of a baron, on paper he is addressed as The Honorable, but you won't be writing to him. Then there is Athene." He paused as if looking for the right words.

"Whose child is Athene?"

"A Greek shipowner's. You've probably seen the name in the papers. She is Athene Paxos."

Dimly the name did mean something to Mrs. Johnstone. It was a name that often turned up in gossip columns. "Why does Athene need you as a guardian?"

"Hermes Paxos has interests and properties all over the world. He is always traveling on business. It breaks his wife's heart that they see so little of Athene but she feels her place is by her husband's side for they entertain a lot. Both parents make a point of seeing that they have Athene with them for the summer holidays, but at Christmas and Easter it is not always possible. Poor Athene doesn't know what a real home is for Hermes Paxos has so many houses that Athene seldom spends long in any of them."

"Poor little girl! How old is she?"

"Eleven. Don't think her parents don't love her. They do, but a man like her father feels he must put business first. They make every effort to see the child. Why, only last term they flew her over to Canada for a weekend, partly that she might launch a ship but largely to have her with them."

Mrs. Johnstone felt weak at the knees. What could a child be like who launched ships during a weekend in Canada?

"Then," said Mr. Crome senior, "there is my problem child. Sophie. Sophie Jones is nine. She was taken into the home of a childless couple when she was a baby. It was a private arrangement through their doctor. They worshiped the child and spoiled her. Then, to their great joy, they had a baby of their own."

"They didn't turn Sophie out, did they?"

"I'm afraid they did. Apparently she was jealous, and pinched and slapped the baby."

"But she'd have got over that."

67

"Of course she would—she was only four—but the parents couldn't see that. They felt badly about Sophie and as the husband was a rich man he settled a very large sum of money on her and appointed us to make arrangements for the welfare of the child. She's been a great trial to us. She's been in five different schools. She ran away from four and the one she is in now won't have her back next term."

"Suppose she runs away from us?"

"Then she runs. Just let us know and, of course, tell the police."

Mrs. Johnstone looked as appalled as she felt. How was she to cope with the heir to a peerage, a millionaire's daughter and a little savage of nine?

"I think if I'd known who the children were I would have refused to move to Caldicott Place. I don't mind telling you I'm scared to death by the whole undertaking."

"Will you tell your children what I have told you about Freddie, Athene and Sophie?"

Mrs. Johnstone thought about that. "I don't think so, certainly not all you've said about Sophie. I want them to get on together and they might be put off."

Nobody was sorry to say good-by to Elstob Buildings, but Mrs. Johnstone was not the only one to be worried about going to Caldicott Place. Nor the only one to be anxious about Freddie, Athene and Sophie.

Bill thought it would be fine to live in Caldicott Place but he could not see how they were going to manage without working like slaves. He had a horrible feeling the Christmas holidays weren't going to be a holiday at all; that it would be one long, "Bill, would you . . ." "Bill, I wonder if . . ." It would not be so bad if he had to slave to help Mum, but he didn't fancy doing it for three strange children, all of them rich and all of them probably spoiled. He did not mind so much about the two strange girls, but he wasn't going to work all hours to make a fat, spoiled Freddie comfortable. If Mum' thought that she had another think coming.

Carol was worried about the move because of her dancing. She was doing well at the new dancing school and didn't want to change again. She had tried to persuade her mother to let her go up to London once a week but she had got no satisfaction.

"Certainly not. I can't make any plans until after the Christmas holiday, but I hope then to hear of someplace at Brighton or Eastbourne where you can learn."

"But I want to go to some holiday classes," Carol protested.

That made her mother cross.

"Do stop thinking only of yourself, Carol. I can't spare you to go to dancing classes this Christmas. I'm relying on you to do things with Athene and Sophie."

Carol did not mean to be selfish but really Mum was being dim. Couldn't she understand that somebody who hoped to be a dancer couldn't just stop learning for several weeks? Of course she could practice on her own but it was risky; it was so easy not to notice some fault, and faults were difficult to cure once you started them. As for Athene and Sophie, Mum seemed to forget it was *her* Christmas holiday, and she didn't mean to spend it looking after two rich girls.

Only Tim had no worries. He had given Jelly a home, a far better one than Jelly could have dreamed of. Sometime after Christmas Dad was coming to live in the lodge at Caldicott Place. Soon he could fish and make a garden and then he'd be well again. "And it'll be my house that made him well. My very own house," Tim told himself. When he thought this he felt sort of swollen inside with being happy.

The family and Jelly moved to Caldicott Place a week before the school holidays began. This proved easy to arrange as all three children were in any case going to new schools the next term.

For the sake of his three wards, Mr. Crome senior was very anxious that the move to Caldicott Place should be a success. But he also wanted it to succeed for the Johnstones' sake.

"I've become interested in the family," he told Jim. "I should like to think of the father being cured thanks to Lady Paine's legacy to Tim. She was such a dear and she would be so pleased."

To help make the move a success Mr. Crome senior suggested to Mrs. Johnstone that Jim should not only drive the family down to Sussex but should stay there for two or three days to help settle them in.

"There are sure to be things that are needed," he said, "so a young man with a car who can fetch and carry will be a help."

"A help!" Mrs. Johnstone gasped. "Bless you, he'll make all the difference. We've all got so fond of him, and I won't feel half so scared of that big place with him there."

Jim did make all the difference. Even with Mrs. Pennywell coming in every day and her daughter coming for an hour or two "when pressed" (which was how her presence was always described), and the daughter's husband Sam coming after work, there was a terrible rush to get that part of the house they would use habitable before the guest children arrived.

The type of furniture that belonged to the house had proved on examination to be of almost no use for small rooms. There were some lovely things, such as chandeliers and huge gilt-edged looking-glasses and some vast furniture, but nothing small. So out of the money advanced by Mr. Crome senior Mrs. Johnstone had ordered what was needed and arranged for it to be delivered on the afternoon before the family arrived, and she had arranged with Mrs. Pennywell to see it in. But when the family drove up to the front door there was no pile of furniture and parcels waiting for them.

"I was here until nearly seven o'clock," Mrs. Pennywell told them, "but it never come. I would have telephoned you, Mr. Jim, but first I didn't have the number and second they haven't turned on the telephone. They put it in last week like they said, and they told me they'd be back to turn it on the next day but they never come. You know what that sort in uniform are."

"Is the hot water all right?" Mrs. Johnstone asked

without much hope.

But Mrs. Pennywell had some good news as well as bad. "Lovely. It was a bit come and go to start with. Then my son-in-law Sam come and had a dekko. I don't know what he did but it's never looked back since."

"Don't worry, Mrs. J.," said Jim. "I'll go down to the village and ring the store to find out why the things haven't arrived, and I'll get the engineers along to fix the telephone."

Jim's telephoning was a success, for the family had only just finished their picnic lunch when the furniture arrived with everything that had been ordered, and it was followed by the telephone engineers.

Mrs. Pennywell watched the men carrying the furniture in as if she were a brigadier general reviewing troops.

"Mind your feet." "Now follow me, I'll show you where to put that bed." "Careful with that table, we don't want it scratched before we've started to use it." Then, to Bill and Carol: "If you undo those parcels you'll find curtains, I shouldn't wonder. My daughter's a wonder at hanging curtains." She turned to Tim. "Hi, you, the village is straight down the lane, and my daughter lives in the cottage next to the church. You can't miss it, there's a green door. You say to my daughter— Edup her name is—'your Mum says if pressed would you come up to The Place right away.' Tell her the curtains has come."

Tim was quite willing to take Jelly for a walk, but he did wish he might open parcels first and help carry things in from the van. But nobody seemed to want him.

"Out of the way, sonny," said the furniture men.

Carol giggled. "I suppose her name's really Edith. Anyway, you go and fetch her, Tim. There's nothing for you to do here."

Bill backed her up. "Yes, off you go. You'll only be in the way."

"Shall Jelly and me take Lady?" Tim asked Jim, for Lady also was staying for two or three days.

"No thanks, old man," said Jim rather vaguely, for he was checking a list of what should be in the van. "She'd have to be on a lead and she pulls so hard she might knock you over."

Tim was rather cross and he told Jelly about it as they walked down the lane.

"You wouldn't think the way they're all behaving that this was my house. You heard them. 'Go and fetch Edup,' Mrs. Pennywell said. And Carol said: 'There's nothing for you to do here,' and when I asked about Lady, which was nice of us, you could see Jim wasn't really listening."

But it was impossible to go on feeling cross as he walked down the lane to the village. Tim saw for the first time a holly tree covered with berries. He stood still to admire it and, as he did so, a thought came to him which almost took his breath away.

"That holly tree is mine, my very own," he told Jelly. "That is the wall of my land and that's where the holly tree is growing. Imagine picking your very own Christmas holly!"

The village was tiny but pretty. There was a village green with a pond on which some ducks were swimming. There was a ring of cottages around the green, each with a garden. There was a village shop; there was a public house called The Caldicott Arms. It had an inn sign with a lion painted on it sitting in a green field. There was a school with a buzz of children reciting coming out of it, and there was the church. Next to the church there was a cottage with a green door. Tim put Jelly on his lead.

"That's where Edup lives," he told him. Then he added: "Oh, Jelly, we are going to like living here."

Edup was a younger edition of her mother—cheerful-looking with a round red-cheeked face.

Tim smiled at her. "I'm Tim. Mrs. Pennywell said to say"—he took a deep breath to be sure he got the message right—"if pressed will you come up to The Place right away. I was to tell you the curtains have come."

"Ah!" said Edup. "You wait here, shan't be a jiff, just put on my coat."

Edup and Tim walked back up the lane together. Tim approved of Edup for she didn't treat him as a child to be kept out of the way, but as the owner of Caldicott Place.

"How does it feel owning a big place like Caldicott?" she asked.

"Well, I think I'll like it, but now that we've got here nobody lets me do anything. You wouldn't know from the way everybody orders me about that it was my house."

Edup thought about that. "I wouldn't trouble myself if I was you. If they like to get your house ready for you it gives you more time to explore like. You know, houses and land are like people—they need knowing before they can be friends."

Tim was surprised. "Do they? I never thought of that. But then, of course, I've always known our own house, and anyway it's not big like Caldicott Place. Do you think it wants to know me?"

"Shouldn't wonder," said Edup. "You visit every square inch and let it know you're pleased to know it and mean to treat it right. You don't want to rush things with property no more than you do with people."

Tim looked respectfully at Edup. "Thank you very much for telling me that. I'll do just what you say and try not to mind if I mayn't help unpack."

7.

The Visitors

By evening the house began to look lived in. All the rooms the family was using, except the smaller of the two drawing rooms, which the children's mother now called the lounge, were behind the green baize door. This had been the servants' quarters. The servants had not been allowed to use the front stairs but had their own back stairs. These came in handy now for the front stairs were wide and would have cost a lot to carpet. But the back stairs were narrow and looked cheerful with the new red carpeting. There was red carpet too along the passage where the bedrooms were. It couldn't be said the stairs or passage were warm, but at least the red made them look warm.

Everybody meant to be good and helpful, but getting the house habitable was tiring, and when people are tired they say and do things they wouldn't say or do ordinarily. Edup, quite by accident, started the first outburst. It was when she saw some cream-colored curtains decorated with rosebuds tied with blue bows.

"Oh, aren't they sweetly pretty! I always fancy rosebuds. I shouldn't wonder if those are for your room, Carol."

There had been so much to do since they arrived that the question of which room each member of the family was to have had not been discussed. Now Mrs. Johnstone, telling the men to which room to carry a carpet, saw the curtains in Edup's arms.

"Don't bother to hang those today. They're for one of the visitors. We must aim just to get our own rooms straight today. Perhaps you'd hang Carol's curtains. She's in the little room at the end of the passage. She's to have those green velvet curtains you altered for me."

Edup had cut those out of some big curtains that had been carefully packed away covered in moth balls. Age had faded the material and there were almost yellow stripes where it had been folded. Carol was disgusted; so she was to be palmed off with faded old curtains smelling of moth balls, was she?

"I suppose that stuck-up Athene is to have the rosebuds."

Too late her mother realized she had been tactless.

"I don't suppose she's stuck-up, poor child, and you do see that the guests must have the new things. I'm using old curtains for us but after the holidays I'll have yours dyed. They are a bit patchy, I'm afraid."

Carol hated herself for behaving badly but since her father's accident she didn't seem able to stop.

"All right. Any old thing is good enough for us, I suppose."

Wisely her mother moved on after the men; nobody could say whether or not she had heard Carol's last remark.

The next day there was a flare-up with Bill. It had been arranged that everybody could, if they wished, have a log fire in their bedrooms.

"But," the children's mother had said, "everybody— and that includes the guests—must look after their own fires, carrying up the logs and clearing the fireplaces."

That first night the log fires had been a great comfort in partially furnished rooms, so the next morning his mother said to Bill:

"Be a dear and bring up some logs and lay and light the fires in the visitors' rooms. They're like refrigerators."

Bill was outraged. "I thought you said we would only

have fires in our bedrooms if we did them ourselves."

"So I did," his mother agreed. "But I do want the rooms reasonably warm when the visitors arrive."

Bill had slaved all the day before and had woken up still tired. To lay those fires did not just mean lumping piles of logs up the stairs, it meant bringing them in from where they were stored and quite possibly sawing up some more. This was just what he had been afraid would happen. Slave, slave, slave all through the Christmas holidays.

"Look, Mum, I don't mind carrying some wood up to the two girls' rooms, but I'm not going to kill myself getting Freddie's room warm. It won't hurt him to be a bit cold. It'll be a change for him, I shouldn't wonder."

His mother too had woken up tired, which made her sound cross. "All right, you lay and light the girls' fires. I'll see to Freddie's fire myself."

Of course Bill could not allow that so he went out and filled a wheelbarrow with logs. But as he stacked them he muttered:

"Fat spoiled beast! If Mum thinks I'm going to wait on him she has another think coming."

Jim was not there that morning or he'd have cheered them all up. He had left early on a secret mission. It was the result of a talk he and Mrs. Johnstone had after the children were in bed.

"You know, Mrs. J., it strikes me there's awfully little for six kids to do in this house. All right when it's fine but what are you going to do with them when the weather's bad?"

That made the children's mother remember all they had left behind in the shed in their garden. She told Jim about it.

"There's masses of stuff. Piles of books. Carol's gramophone and records, a lot of chemistry things belonging to Bill, and the biggest railway set you ever did see belonging to Tim."

That gave Jim an idea.

"You know that room that on the blueprint of the house is grandly called the Servant's Hall? Well, why don't you turn that into a playroom? It's got a big table and a bookshelf. We could get a table-tennis outfit and when the television set comes we could put it in there, plus Tim's train set and so on."

From there it was only a step to deciding to get the playroom ready in secret, and so give the children—especially Tim—a surprise.

"You leave it to me, Mrs. J.," Jim said. "I'll nip off early and fetch all the stuff from your house. Then I'll go to a store and pick out a table-tennis set and anything else I think will come in handy. Don't worry about expense. All the children have allowances for amusements."

Jim came back about teatime and parked his loaded station wagon in one of the garages.

"Got everything, Mrs. J.," he whispered. "You wait until you see the stuff. I'll bring it in tonight and we'll fix up the room. I'll love to see the children's faces tomorrow morning."

Jim was certainly a wonderful shopper. He had

80

bought not only the table-tennis outfit but all the newest games and a vast jigsaw puzzle. As well, he'd remembered the shortage of furniture so there were some chairs, a folding table and a special small table for Carol's record player. He and the children's mother had great fun arranging the room. Jim especially enjoyed laying out Tim's train set.

"But," said Mrs. Johnstone, "I've not put the TV in here. It came today and it's fixed up in the lounge. This will be the children's room. If they want to watch TV they can watch it in the lounge."

It was decided that after breakfast the next morning the children would be introduced to the playroom.

"Though it's probably a mistake," said the children's mother. "Once they've seen it I shall have a job getting them out of it to help with the rest of the house."

It is miserable to hope to give people a pleasant surprise and find they are not pleased at all. When Bill, Carol and Tim were shown the playroom they were horrified.

Tim said: "I don't want my train set here. I'll have it in my bedroom. If it's here those children that are coming might touch it."

The children's mother was going to tell Tim not to be selfish, but Jim stopped her.

"I never thought of that," he said cheerfully. "I've got some odd jobs to do but after that I'll help you carry it up to your room."

Carol was delighted to see her record player and records again, but it was not going to be common property. If that Athene turned out to be all right she could be invited to listen to the records in her bedroom.

"I'm afraid, Mum, I'll have to take my record player to my room. It has to be looked after. If Sophie messes about with it, which she might—after all she's only nine —it will be out of order in a day."

Jim thought it was only too likely Sophie would mess about with the record player, especially if she was told not to, and he blamed himself for not thinking of it.

"Too right, Carol," he agreed. "I'll help you cart it up."

Bill felt ashamed of his outburst the day before but he really couldn't have his precious chemistry things in a children's playroom.

"I'm not being dog-in-the-manger but I'm afraid I'm moving my chemistry stuff. This is a splendid room for games but you can't have valuable stuff about in the same room you're playing table tennis."

When the children had gone to their rooms carrying their belongings Jim and Mrs. Johnstone looked at each other.

"Oh dear!" she said. "What have I taken on? It's not like my children to be selfish. When we were at home the house was always full of their friends. They have never got over their father's accident."

"Don't fuss, Mrs. J. It will all come out in the wash. You wait until I bring our three kids down on Tuesday and you'll see."

"Oh, how I hope you're right! But there's so much to do before then and I do want to have everything nice for them."

"I don't see why you should take my advice," said Jim, "but I'm giving it all the same. I wouldn't have everything too finished—you know, Christmas decorations and all that. I think you'll find our wards will enjoy being allowed to help. Just treat them as family."

Tuesday was a beast of a day. It was bitterly cold with an icy wind and driving rain. But inside the house it was cheerful. There were log fires in every room the family was using, and there was a holly wreath on the front door. In the hall there was a vast Christmas tree which had been chosen by the children and cut down by Sam. The children had wanted to decorate the tree.

"It'll look so gay and welcoming," Carol had pleaded.

But her mother remembered what Jim had said.

"Put a few colored lights on if you like but we'll decorate it properly when the other children are here to help. It'll give them something to do while they're settling in."

It was teatime when the children, watching from the window, saw the lights of Jim's car turn in at the gates.

"They're here," Carol shouted.

The whole family and Jelly rushed to the front door.

Afterwards it was difficult to remember how the visitors had looked that first afternoon. Athene was wearing a cream-colored fur coat with a matching fur hat. They all remembered that. Freddie looked extraordinarily small for somebody of twelve and, far from being fat as Bill had imagined him, he was so thin you would think he never got enough to eat. Nobody remembered how Sophie had looked that first day but they never forgot what she had said. The children's mother was kissing Athene.

"A merry Christmas, dear. I do hope you will be happy staying here."

Sophie strutted forward, her chin in the air. "I don't suppose I'll be happy but if I don't like it here I'll run away. I always do."

"A lovable child is Sophie," said Jim. "A daily beating is what she needs, Mrs. J."

Carol showed Athene up to her room. Bill was told to take charge of Freddie and Tim of Sophie. Both Bill and Carol were surprised by their charges. Athene, in spite of her rich clothes, seemed very unpretentious. Carol, waiting for criticism, got none. Athene seemed enchanted with everything.

"What a pretty room! Imagine being you and living here always."

"We haven't," Carol explained. "We've only been here a week and we've worked like slaves to get the house even as much in order as it is."

Tea was ready so Athene took off her coat. She was wearing a simple brown frock. It might have cost a lot of money but it looked like many of the frocks in Carol's wardrobe.

Athene looked in approval at Carol's jeans and pullover. "I hoped we'd wear that sort of clothes here. I do hate dressing up, don't you?"

"You can't dress up here except for something special like Christmas Day—there's such an awful lot to do." Carol nodded at the fire. "That's lit for you today but if we want fires in our rooms—and of course we do for there's no central heating—we have to see to them ourselves: fetch the logs, clear the fireplace, everything."

Athene's eyes shone. "How gorgeous! I'll like doing that."

Carol just couldn't adjust herself to this Athene who was so different from the girl she had imagined.

"Come on," she said. "I'll show you the bathroom and then you'd better come down to tea."

Bill was finding Freddie equally surprising; far from throwing his weight about he was—Bill couldn't think of the exact word to describe him—meek was the nearest he could get. Freddie was not only small and thin himself but he spoke in a nervous small voice.

"I'm sorry Sophie was rude to your mother. She's nothing to us, you know. Athene and I, I mean. We only met her once before when we were all taken to winter sports."

"What was she like then?" Bill asked.

"We didn't see much of her. Both Athene and I can ski but she was only beginning. We just met her at meals. We didn't bother with her much."

Bill wondered if Freddie was afraid of being overheard. "You needn't whisper. The walls are pretty thick and Sophie's room is across the passage."

Freddie flushed. "I'm awfully sorry. It's just habit. You see, until I was eight I lived with my grandfather. He only took me as a duty because my father had to live in Australia. When I came home for the holidays he gave orders I was to be kept out of his way, so I got into the habit of creeping about and whispering."

Bill was shocked. "The old beast!"

"Not really. He liked having his house to himself. Why should he want a little boy shoved on him? And I was very little when I first lived with him."

"If your father is in Australia why don't you live with him?"

Freddie sounded surprised at the question. "Why should he want me? He's got a new family now. I think he pretty well hates me because I have to inherit the title and not his son by my stepmother."

Bill was knocked speechless. Here was he expecting a spoiled, fat Freddie and instead there had arrived a thin, almost ill-treated Freddie.

"The bathroom's just up the passage," he said. "Come down to tea when you're ready. There's a smashing motor racing game done with magnets. Jim bought it —I'll show it to you afterwards."

Tim was furious with Sophie. How dare she speak like that to Mum!

"This is your room," he said, throwing open the door. "The fire was lit by Bill but after today you'll have to do it yourself."

Sophie took off her coat while she looked around her room.

"It'll do," she said in a grand voice. "It's not rooms and things like that which make me run away—it's people."

Tim could have hit her.

"I shan't mind if you run away—in fact I think I'd

like it. Mum said to tell you the bathroom is next door and when you've washed come down because tea's ready. She said she'd help you unpack afterwards."

In spite of the bad start with Sophie, and the children's father being in the hospital, it was a good Christmas on the whole. It started off well for during the night after the visitors arrived it snowed. In the morning Mrs. Pennywell arrived, even redder-cheeked than usual, pulling a sledge.

"This was Edup's when she was young," she told Mrs. Johnstone. "We want holly and logs for the house and things from the shop, so I thought the kids could get the lot while you and me straighten up."

This meant that the children had a busy and an entertaining morning, for who would not enjoy cutting his own holly and bringing it home on a sledge, singing "Good King Wenceslaus" to a barked accompaniment from a wildly excited Jelly?

It was fun too doing the shopping. The village shop seemed to sell everything; besides the usual groceries and fruit there were boots hanging from the ceiling and medicines for animals as well as human beings. The shop was also the post office; the whole business was run by an old lady called Mrs. Binding, with the help of a little grandson called Alfie.

"Only helps in the holidays and of an evening Alfie does," she told the children. "But very useful he is."

The children could not imagine how Mrs. Binding managed during term time for she depended on Alfie for so much.

"Self-raising flour," she said, looking at Mrs. Penny-well's list. "Top shelf, Alfie, on the left; you'll need the ladder. Six dozen oranges. Better get a case out from the back, Alfie, and while you're at it better put it on the sledge. You boys will give him a hand, won't you? Biscuits mixed, better send a tin. It's the one on the top, Alfie; put it on the sledge."

Because there was only the one sledge, the children did all that had to be done together, and also worked together in the afternoon, first decorating the house with the holly and ivy they had picked, and then, with Mrs. Johnstone's help, decorating the tree. But already there were signs that they would pair up. It was, of course, natural for Freddie and Bill to get together and for Carol and Athene to do so, but this left Tim and Sophie and that did not work.

It was after tea that the first sign of trouble occurred. Carol, meaning to be friendly, lit the fire in her bedroom and invited Athene up to hear her records. As it was snowing hard, Bill asked Freddie to come out with him to the garage with the sledge so they could stack logs outside the back door where everyone could get them without getting wet. Tim, without saying anything to anybody, went up to his bedroom with Jelly to play with his model railway. This, of course, left Sophie on her own.

Mrs. Johnstone was in the lounge sitting down for the first time that day when the door opened and Sophie came in. At once Mrs. Johnstone put on what she hoped was a welcoming smile.

"Hullo, Sophie. Come to watch the telly?"

"I don't know where everybody is. They've just gone. People are always mean to me."

Mrs. Johnstone tried hard to forget how much she disliked children who whined and to think only about poor Sophie being turned out by the people who nearly adopted her.

"Never mind, I'm sure there's something nice on the telly. Let's look and see, shall we?"

"I don't want to watch television, I want someone to play with. Where's Tim?"

Mrs. Johnstone quite clearly in her mind's eye saw Tim lying on his tummy playing with his trains, and though she did not want to entertain Sophie she was not going to disturb him. He had worked hard all day and deserved some time to himself.

"I don't know," she said. "Shall we go to the playroom and find something to amuse you?"

"I'd rather just sit here and talk."

There was nothing Mrs. Johnstone felt less like just then than sitting and talking. Still, Sophie was a visitor and perhaps feeling lonely and strange, so she gave in. But though she tried hard to sound enthusiastic she did not succeed very well.

"How nice! Come and sit by the fire. What shall we talk about?"

Sophie settled herself in a chair facing her hostess.

"What I like talking about," she said, "is me." And for the next hour she did just that.

8.
Problems

After Christmas Mrs. Johnstone had to be away a lot.
The doctor at the hospital had said:

"I think you should try and visit your husband at
least every other day. I know you are planning that he
should for the time being live alone in the lodge, but

you will, of course, see him a lot so it is important he gets accustomed to having you around."

It was an hour-and-a-half journey by bus to the hospital, so every other day Mrs. Johnstone left soon after breakfast and did not return until tea-time. This meant that she had to leave Bill and Mrs. Pennywell in charge. It worried her.

"I don't like being out so much," she told Bill. "Athene's all right but Sophie needs looking after or she might run away."

Bill thought Sophie a bore and that her running away would be good news, except that it would add to his mother's worries.

"Don't fuss, we'll look after her."

"Then there's the lodge," said his mother. "Edup's Sam is, as you know, painting the outside of the place and Edup when pressed is giving it a good cleaning inside, but the sitting room and bedroom need a coat of paint. Do you think you could manage that?"

"O.K., and I know Freddie will help."

His mother gave a sort of laugh. It was, she thought, almost embarrassing the way Freddie and Athene helped —so noticeably more willingly than her own children.

"I'm sure he will. Anyway I'm leaving you in charge when I'm out but Mrs. Pennywell will be here all day, so if you want any advice you can rely on her."

"Don't worry," said Bill, "everything will be all right."

Mrs. Pennywell certainly was a pillar of strength for she never seemed to allow things to worry her.

"What can't be mended must be endured," she was

fond of saying. She was interested in the children but she was not a believer in interfering.

"If children want something they'll ask fast enough."

One morning she was proved right. She was making a steak and kidney pie for lunch when Carol wandered in and sat on the edge of the kitchen table. Mrs. Pennywell smiled welcomingly.

"Hullo, dear! On your own?"

"Everybody's gone out and left me," said Carol. "Bill and Freddie are painting the lodge. Athene's doing the shopping and she's taken Sophie with her."

Mrs. Pennywell looked up from the pastry she was making. "Oh, that was kind."

Carol gave her a funny look. "Athene's always kind and good. Haven't you noticed?"

"No harm in being either," Mrs. Pennywell retorted. "Where's young Tim?"

"Going around the place like he does every day. He says he's getting to know it. Edup said he ought to." Carol pulled a small piece off the pastry. "Do you like music, Mrs. Pennywell?"

Mrs. Pennywell gave her pastry a slap. "Not if it's those Beatles and such, but I fancy a nice tune when I've got a chance to hear one."

Carol rolled the pastry around in the palms of her hands. "At home all the girls liked pop music. One girl liked it so much she sort of fainted. I didn't know any girl didn't like it."

"And who doesn't?"

Carol began making a rabbit out of her piece of pastry.

"Athene. I asked her up to hear my pop music the day after she came. Well, she sat and listened but she didn't rave. So I asked: 'Don't you like music?' and do you know what she said? 'Not this sort much. I like classical.' Imagine!"

Mrs. Pennywell put an egg cup upside down in the center of the pie dish and fixed her pastry over it.

"It's always the same, dear. Pennywell, before he was took—food-poisoning it was, a pie he ate at an outing—well, he was crazy about that wrestling on the telly, which I can't abide. What I like is a good serial—same people each time so you know where you are. Well, we've only got one room so nothing could be done. Mr. Pennywell saw his wrestling and I saw my serials but we never watched together. We never thought less of each other, though."

Carol shaped her rabbit's ears. "But that's different—you're old. Athene's nearly the same age as me, so you'd expect her to be with it."

Mrs. Pennywell put her pie in the oven. "She's been brought up different from you."

Carol threw her rabbit on the table. "That's got nothing to do with it. Princess Anne's been brought up differently from me but I bet she plays pop music and is mad about it."

"Well, you and Athene must agree to differ, musn't you?" said Mrs. Pennywell comfortably. "What can't be cured must be endured."

Carol kicked at a leg of the table. "I think I've endured too much lately."

Mrs. Pennywell sat down to peel potatoes. "How's that, dear?"

"I don't suppose you understand any more than Mum does, but it's my dancing. I was getting on, I know I was. I think Miss Rome thought I just might be good enough to be professional—you know, dance in shows and things. She never said so but that's what the other girls thought. Well, when we moved to London I went to a very good place though I didn't like it so much as at Miss Rome's, but here nothing's fixed." Carol's voice wobbled. "Mum said she couldn't make any plans until the holidays were over, then she'd find somewhere, probably in Eastbourne." She gave the table leg another kick. "Probably in Eastbourne! As if it didn't matter whom I learned with. You see, if I go to the wrong place it could ruin my whole future."

Mrs. Pennywell had never seen a ballet class so she had no idea what Carol was talking about, but she could see that Carol thought what she was saying was important.

"Don't fret, dear. The holidays will soon be over. Then, as soon as your Dad's settled in, something proper will be fixed. You'll see."

"Something ought to be fixed now," said Carol. "You can't muck about with dancing. I'd write and ask Miss Rome whom I should learn with but it's no good in the Christmas holidays because she has special classes every day. She wouldn't have time to answer."

Mrs. Pennywell laid down her potato peeler. "It's upsetting I can see, dear, but worriting won't help."

"Nobody does anything I like doing. Oh, Mrs. Pennywell, if only you knew how gorgeous everything was when Dad was well and we lived at home. You see, I'd heaps of friends who came in, and sometimes we went to films."

Mrs. Pennywell laughed. "Proper town miss you are. Well, why don't you help Bill and Freddie get the lodge ready?"

"I expect you despise me but I hate the smell of paint."

"Well, you could have gone shopping with Athene and Sophie."

Carol got off the table. "I suppose you're right and I'm the town type. I don't like walking about in the country. I thought it was loathsome in London because I had to share a room with Mum. Now I've got a room to myself but the house if stuffed with visitors and I'm afraid I don't like it. I'm sure you think I'm horrible but I wasn't when Dad was well and we lived at home. Truly I wasn't."

Mrs. Pennywell gave Carol a comforting smile. "I don't think you're horrible or anything like it. You've been upset and you've got growing pains, but you'll get over it."

"Will I? Oh, I am glad! You see, I know when I'm beastly and then I hate myself for being mean to Mum."

Mrs. Pennywell had finished the last potato. "I expect your Mum understands. Now off you go and get a breath of air or you won't have worked up an appetite for my pie."

Carol was not the only one who talked to Mrs.

Pennywell. Freddie often came into the kitchen for a talk. Though she was fond of him, Mrs. Pennywell thought he was a strange boy.

"Like an old man sometimes," she confided to Edup. "You'd think he was the father of a family the way he carries on."

"Shocking the way he's afraid to speak up," said Edup.

"Too right." Mrs. Pennywell agreed. "If he wasn't dead already I could strangle that old grandfather of his who made him that way. Though, mind you, Freddie's getting better with mixing with our Bill. Twice lately I've heard him shout—or as near as he can get to a shout."

"We don't need to worry much about young Fred," Edup said. "As you know, when pressed I go to the lodge to wash the floors and all that. Well, the boys are painting down below and to hear the way they carry on you'd think they'd known each other all their lives."

It was true. For Freddie the holiday was turning out to be a wonderful success. What he most enjoyed was the feeling of being wanted, and only he knew just how badly he was needed. Bill had agreed to paint the lodge but, left to himself, the work would have gone on slowly for there were so many other things he wanted to do. But Freddie was a sticker. Every morning he marched off to the lodge as if he were going to business, and he saw to it that Bill came with him.

"Get this finished and I'll ask your mother if I can hire some horses," he promised, "and I'll teach you to ride."

To hear them talking a stranger would have thought Freddie was the son of the house and Bill the visitor.

"I do think it's awfully tiring for your mother going by bus to the hospital," Freddie would whisper in a worried voice.

"It's not for long," said Bill. "I shouldn't wonder if they let Dad come here at the end of the month."

"She looks so tired when she gets home. And then she cooks our supper."

Bill was puzzled. "Of course she cooks our supper. Who else?" Then he laughed. "Don't tell Mrs. Penny-well you think Mum's tired when she gets home, because Athene told her and she said"—he gave a fair imitation of Mrs. Pennywell's voice—" 'Mrs. Johnstone's lucky to have a husband to visit. You look at me. All I can do for mine is put a wreath on his grave.' "

Freddie paid no attention. "I wish we had a car for your mother."

Bill pretended to punch him. "You are a fat-head! Who'd drive a car if we had it? Mum can't."

But Freddie went on worrying. "I wish Jim Crome would come down again. He'd think of something—he always does."

The child who fascinated Mrs. Pennywell was Athene. The housekeeper had read about her millionaire father in the newspaper and she knew the girl had at least six homes. To her she had much in common with a fairy-tale character like The Sleeping Beauty. She could have understood if Athene had flounced about and given

97

orders, but that was not the way she behaved. What Athene loved was to be allowed to do housework.

"First time it happened I thought it was just a bit of fun for her, so I gave in to her," Mrs. Pennywell confided to Edup. "But it's gone on. I can understand a girl giving a helping hand when she has to—well, you did yourself—but I never knew one that thought helping a treat. But that's how Athene sees it."

In the end Mrs. Pennywell had to accept the fact that Athene really liked helping.

Then one morning when she was helping with the washing up Athene tried to explain about herself.

"You see, it's fun for me doing what I'm never allowed to do. I never go into the kitchen of any of our houses —there's always masses of servants. I think there'd be a riot if they even caught me using a duster."

Mrs. Pennywell could not imagine what Athene's homes were like, but hearing about them was like reading a glossy magazine.

"Got your own room in all the houses I suppose, dear, and done up ever so pretty, I expect."

Athene knew what Mrs. Pennywell liked to hear; so she told her all about her homes and the yacht.

"My mother is awfully good at decorating and she tries extra hard with my rooms because she can't see me all the time. She often says she wishes she could cut herself in half so she could be half with me and half with Daddy."

"Pity your Dad can't manage to get home for your holidays."

Athene struggled to explain. "Well, you can't be a person like him and just leave your business. He's a gorgeous father when I do see him. But, always moving about the way I do, you can see how heavenly I find it staying here."

"There's many might fancy your life. Young Carol, for one."

"But why? Imagine knowing you'd go back to the same house every holiday, to the same room, finding all your things just where you'd left them. That's my idea of heaven, Mrs. Pennywell."

"Well, I'm glad of extra hands, no saying I'm not, though what your Pa and Ma would say I can't imagine."

Because they needed an eye kept on them, Tim and Sophie came under Mrs. Pennywell's care when Mrs. Johnstone was at the hospital. Sophie, difficult though she was in most ways, needed no encouragement to keep herself clean and tidy. She was a pretty child with wonderful blue-gray eyes and fair hair. She knew she was pretty so she took trouble with herself, brushing her hair until it shone, and always appearing at meals with clean hands. She was different from Tim, who always had to be herded toward washing.

"Let's look at these hands, Tim," Mrs. Pennywell would say before every meal.

Tim felt that passing his hands under a running tap was more than sufficient washing for anyone.

"They may look rather gray," he would protest, "but it's clean earth which is quite different from London dirt."

"Whatever it is, up to the bathroom and let's get it off," Mrs. Pennywell would retort.

It was while he was washing that Tim would pour out to Mrs. Pennywell an account of his day's doings.

"Today Jelly and me went to a new place. Edup said I was to visit every square inch so my land would know I was pleased to meet it and meant to treat it right."

Mrs. Pennywell would roll back Tim's jersey sleeves. "Those wrists can do with a good wash too. Edup's right —just owning a place is nothing. It's knowing it that matters."

Each day Tim was full of questions. "What would little tiny green leaves be in a sort of ring? They grow under the dead leaves."

"Wait and see is my motto. A celandine maybe or could be a primrose."

"When Dad comes he won't need to make a garden —everything seems to come up wild. At home we planted primroses."

Mrs. Pennywell would pass the towel to Tim. "Fond of your Dad, aren't you?"

"Of course. But I haven't seen him for simply ages. Mum says when he comes we aren't to bother him to begin with, that he wants to live alone. But I bet that isn't true."

Mrs. Pennywell thought it unlikely too. However, the children's mother had told her that was what the doctor wanted.

"If your Mum says it's true, it's true. We must just hope he picks up quickly."

Problems

Bill and Mrs. Pennywell got together to discuss problems, especially the daily problem of Sophie. Nobody really wanted to do things with Sophie so something had to be arranged. Usually Bill's talks with Mrs. Pennywell took place the moment his mother had left for the hospital. The opening was always much the same.

"I suppose there's nothing you are doing which Sophie could help with, is there, Mrs. Pennywell?"

The answer was usually: "No, dear, there isn't. There's a lot to do in this house and young Sophie's a born hindrance."

Bill tried to divide Sophie fairly between them all but Mrs. Pennywell was right—Sophie was a born hindrance. Instead of doing whatever she was supposed to be doing, all she did was talk, and always about herself. It did not matter whether Freddie and Bill took her to the lodge to help with the painting or Mrs. Pennywell found something for her to do in the kitchen, or Athene took her shopping, or Tim took her around the property, or Carol tried to amuse her. The result was always the same.

Her talk was usually a hard-luck story told in a whine. Her favorite was about the Mummy and Daddy who had meant to adopt her and had turned her out because of a new baby. There was no suggestion in Sophie's version that she had behaved badly to the baby, and her story always finished the same way.

"And that Mummy and Daddy who nearly adopted me have missed me ever since. They want me to go back but I never, never will."

There were other stories.

"At that school there was a girl who loved me and wanted me to be her sister. She gave me masses of presents and then people got jealous because she loved me more than anyone else, and they pretended she hadn't given me any presents at all. Anyway I wouldn't stay at that school. I ran away.

"At my last but one school all the mistresses loved me, especially the headmistress; she told me she wanted me for her own little girl. Then the rest of the school got hateful to me. That's why I ran away from that school."

Sophie never got any hand holding from the Johnstone children, who didn't believe in sloppy goings-on. Athene, though she did not understand Sophie, did not mind being clung to on walks to the village, for in Greece outward signs of affection were not thought as sloppy as they were in England. But the drawback to being kind to Sophie was that she expected, once you had shown her affection, that she would get it all the time, and in increasing doses. In fact what Sophie hoped was that the person who was kind would love her and nobody else.

From that evening when Sophie had sat and talked to her, Mrs. Johnstone had realized that she was a child in need of an outward show of affection and she had meant to give it to her. But her life made it difficult. She was as tired as Freddie guessed she was when she got home from the hospital. Even with Mrs. Pennywell around all day Caldicott Place took a lot of running.

Problems were always waiting for her. The minor worries were endless. Then there was the major worry, which she was for the moment keeping to herself.

Her husband seemed no better at all. She had told him about Caldicott Place. She had told him about the lodge, the garden he could make, the fishing. She had told him about the paying-guest children which made living in Caldicott Place possible. Never once had he shown one spark of interest; to her, in spite of what the doctors said, he was just as ill mentally as when he had first regained consciousness. But his doctor did not agree. Then one day he startled her.

"I've good news for you. You can take your husband home next week."

Next week! The last week of the holidays! How, with six children in the house, was she to give the patient the quiet he needed? The elder children would co-operate of course, but what about Tim, and what about Sophie?

9.
Where are you going, my pretty maids?

Mrs. Johnstone told the four elder children her news the day before the patient was to return. After Tim and Sophie were in bed she asked the others to join her in the lounge.

"I am going to treat you as family," she said to Freddie

and Athene. "You've heard about my husband so you know he had a knock on the head and needs time to adjust. The doctor says it is all right for him to be alone. That's the reason you've been helping to get the lodge ready. I'm bringing him home tomorrow."

Bill whistled. "Tomorrow! It's a bit of luck the lodge is finished. I hadn't thought he'd be allowed out for some days yet."

His mother shuddered inwardly at "allowed out." It made it sound as if her husband had been locked up.

"I had a look at the lodge today," she said. "You've done a wonderful job. I congratulate you and Freddie. Bill, the painting is very well done."

"That's mostly Freddie," said Bill honestly. "He's much better at it than I am."

Freddie's voice was still low but it was much stronger. "Sam's done a fine job on the outside and Edup, when pressed, has scrubbed like mad."

"I know," Mrs. Johnstone agreed. "But here's the problem. The doctor wants him to arrive as quietly as possible, just seeing me that first day. How can I make Tim and Sophie grasp this? Or can we keep it from them that he's arriving tomorrow?"

The children looked at one another. Tim was like quicksilver—nobody ever knew where he was. Sophie was always within sight. But if she knew that Mr. Johnstone had arrived at the lodge wouldn't she be only too likely to slip off to see if he would make a good audience for the stories of her wrongs?

"I'm sure we daren't tell Tim," Bill said. "If he knew

Dad was coming, no matter what you said he'd be sure to hang about. I mean, look how he tried to get into the hospital."

"Have any of you any plans for tomorrow afternoon?" Mrs. Johnstone asked.

"Freddie is giving me a riding lesson," said Bill.

"I was going to Edup in the afternoon to learn to make marmalade," said Athene. "But I could put it off."

Mrs. Johnstone looked at Freddie. "Just tomorrow could you give Tim a riding lesson too?"

Bill was secretly disgusted but Freddie was glad to help. "Of course, Mrs. Johnstone. I'll ring the stables in the morning and see if I can get hold of another pony."

They all looked at Carol.

"Could you do something with Sophie, darling?" Mrs. Johnstone asked. "I hate to bother you but you do see somebody has to look after her."

Carol could only nod for she had a lump in her throat which made it hard to speak. She had, though no one knew it, screwed herself up to having a real talk with her mother that night. She had realized her father was soon coming to the lodge, and of course she was glad. But once he was there it would be hard to get her mother to think of anyone else. Now he was coming tomorrow. The new term was less than a week away and they had not even secured the name of a good dancing teacher, let alone begun to make arrangements.

"Have a talk with Mrs. Pennywell," her mother went on. "She was telling me there's a bus goes to a cinema somewhere. If the film is suitable you might take Sophie to that."

The talk became general after that so nobody noticed how silent Carol had become. Nor did anyone think it odd when she gave her mother a kiss and said she was going up to bed. Carol often went up early for she liked playing records before she went to sleep.

But Carol did not play her record player that night. Instead she got out her second most valued possession. It was an album of photographs of dancers, starting with a beautiful one of Margot Fonteyn. Slowly she turned over the pages while she sobbed with self-pity.

"Nobody cares what happens to me. It's not Mum's fault, I suppose. She's fussed to death about Dad. But Dad would care if he was well. When you think that I might dance like the girls in this book if only I had the chance—well perhaps not like them exactly but anyway be a good dancer. Instead they stick me away in the country where I can't get near a dancing teacher. I wouldn't be surprised if nothing's ever fixed all next term. Mum's quite likely to say I can't go into East-bourne on Saturdays, and if the best teacher turns out to be in Brighton I bet she makes me go to one in Eastbourne because it'll be cheaper if I use the pass the Council gives me. Oh, I'm so miserable I could die!"

Once having started to cry Carol couldn't stop. She cried about everything. Missing all her friends. Living in a square world where no one understood pop music or the funny feelings it gave you when it was played. Having to waste all her Christmas holidays helping to look after three strange children. The misery which gnawed at her all the time because of Dad; suppose, oh just suppose he never got well! She had never said this to anyone but sometimes she thought her mother believed Dad would never get well. Then there was her dancing. Of course it was a difficult world to get into, she wasn't a fool. All she wanted was to be properly trained. Then she'd get a job as a dancer even if it wasn't in ballet. You didn't say a thing like that to a ballet teacher, who would have a fit. But she knew she could be perfectly happy with a good troupe. And now, because of Dad's accident and Tim's horrible house, her whole future was to be wrecked.

While she cried Carol heard the others come up to bed. She heard them call out good-night and the bathroom door opening and shutting. She heard her mother softly open her door and whisper, "Asleep, darling?" and getting no reply creep out again. Then she heard her mother's door shut.

Having worked herself up Carol found it hard to get to sleep. There was an old grandfather clock, inherited with the house, in the passage downstairs. She heard it strike eleven and then twelve. "My goodness!" she thought. "I must go to sleep. Perhaps if I had something to eat I'd feel sleepier."

Carol put on her dressing gown and slippers and on tiptoe crept down the stairs to the kitchen. There she found a big box of biscuits. She was just opening it when she was startled by a sound. She swung around expecting to see her mother. But it wasn't her mother, it was Sophie, dressed in a thick coat, fur-lined boots, a scarf tied over her head, and carrying a suitcase.

"Sophie! Where are you going?" Carol exclaimed.

Sophie closed the door so their voices would not be heard. "I'm running away."

"Why?"

"Nobody loves me here. I thought your mother did but tonight she talked to all of you and she shut me out."

"What nonsense! You were in bed, so was Tim."

"I wasn't. I came down to see what was going on. And I'm glad I did because now I know. Your mother talked about me in a horrid way." Sophie imitated Mrs. Johnstone. " 'Could you do something with Sophie, darling? I hate to bother you but you do see somebody has to look after her.' "

Carol flushed. "Listeners hear no good of themselves," she said.

"I never hear good of myself in this house. That's why I'm running away."

"Where to?"

"London. Perhaps I'll go abroad from there."

London! As Sophie spoke Carol suddenly realized that London was not far from where she used to live. A few minutes' talk with Miss Rome, and everything would be settled. If she left now with Sophie she could be home before Mum came back from the hospital with Dad.

"Have you any money, Sophie?"

"Heaps."

"Enough to pay my fare to London as well as yours?"

"Yes."

Carol was so pleased she gave Sophie a sudden hug. "Good. Wait here while I get some clothes on. We're going to London together."

When Carol stepped into the pitch-black driveway with Sophie she suddenly realized that she had no idea where they were going. Hating the country as she did, she never went farther from the house than she had to. She supposed there must be a railway station because they were to have passes to take them into Eastbourne to school. Or were they passes for buses? Now that she came to think about it she had never asked.

"Can I hold your hand?" Sophie asked. "It's awfully dark."

Carol was quite glad to hold Sophie's hand for it certainly was dark and bogey-ish in the drive. As she took her hand she gave it a squeeze.

"Give me your case. I'll carry it."

Sophie was amazed. "Thank you. That's the first time you've been nice to me." Carol was not listening because she was puzzling how to find out where they were going without admitting she did not know how to get to London. After all, she was much the elder so she ought to be in charge. She managed to sound as if she were a walking time-table of trains and buses.

"How were you going to London?"

There were no flies on Sophie. She guessed Carol had no idea how they were going.

"There's a train that takes milk. Mrs. Binding at the shop told me about it. At least she told Athene and I heard."

"What did she say?"

"Well, Athene was saying how good Alfie was and then Mrs. Binding said as a reward she was taking him for a day to London before school began. Well, I was already thinking about running away so I asked her how she went to London."

"What did she say?"

Sophie was good at imitating voices. " 'It'll be a bit early for you, Sophie. We catch a milk train at Winsford Halt at half-past two in the morning. It stops at every station picking up milk.' "

Carol knew vaguely where Winsford Halt was. Just before you got to the village there was a signpost by a stile on which was written "To Winsford Halt." She had supposed it was no longer a working station. Surely Sophie wasn't thinking of crossing that frightening empty field in the dark. There might be some of those awful cows about who could easily turn out to be bulls. However, she tried to sound casual.

"Do you think we can find our way across that field in the dark?"

Sophie was scornful at such foolishness. "It's obvious you've never lived in the country. That's a footpath to the station but of course we won't go that way in the dark. We'll go by the main road. It's a bit longer but we've got heaps of time."

Carol was annoyed by Sophie's tone but it was not the moment to say anything. Sophie might be only nine but she was in charge for it was she who knew the way. Besides, Sophie had to buy the tickets; all the visiting children had a lot of money but Carol had almost nothing left after buying Christmas presents. Then it was terribly important not to quarrel with Sophie, for somewhere between here and London Carol had to persuade her not to run away but to come back with her to Caldicott Place.

As if she could read her thoughts Sophie said: "I don't think your mother will fuss when she finds I've gone. I expect Mr. Crome senior warned her I would run away, and I told her I would if I didn't like it here."

They were out of the driveway and walking up the road. Alone with Sophie—apparently the only people awake in the night world—Carol felt an unexpected comradeship with her and a first pricking of conscience. Would her mother think she had encouraged Sophie?

"It's a pity always to run away because nobody gets a chance to know you long enough to like you."

It seemed as if the anonymity of the night made Sophie more truthful about herself than usual, and for once she didn't whine.

"Absolutely honestly, Carol, I don't think my staying longer would make that happen. I think there is something about me which makes people not like me much."

Carol thought "how true" but this was not the moment to say a thing like that.

"Well, you don't give people a chance. You haven't given us a chance. I mean, you've not been with us three weeks."

Sophie's voice took on her usual whine. "A person like you can't understand a person like me. You can be as hateful as you like but your father and mother and Bill and Tim have to love you because you're family. But nobody has to love me."

Put that way Carol felt miserable. Did her family only love her because they had to? She had been pretty horrible lately.

"I'm afraid you could be right. But there are people who are loved by people who don't have to love them. I mean, look at Freddie."

"Oh, Freddie!" Sophie dismissed him as if he did not count. "He's pleased with anything. He likes people being pleased with him and doesn't expect anything. But I want to belong somewhere, and I'll go on running away and running away until I find a place to belong to."

Carol did not answer at once. But as she trudged along the road she held Sophie's hand more tightly. Sophie was just as full of talk about herself as usual, but for the first time Carol wondered if they all—and herself especially—had been as nice to her as they could have been. At last, just as the lights of Winsford Halt began to glow in the distance, she blurted out:

"You might give us another chance. Now that you've explained, I feel quite differently about you."

Sophie stood stock-still. "Really? Absolutely truthfully?"

"Absolutely truthfully," Carol promised.

"All right. I'll go back," said Sophie. "I'll give you another try."

That was the first time Carol realized that *she* had not explained why she was going to London.

"Would you mind, now that we're almost at the Halt, coming to London with me? You see, when you said where you were going I decided to come too—partly of course to look after you, but also because I want to see my dancing teacher."

"I don't see what good my coming will do," Sophie objected. "If I'm going back I'm going now."

Carol knew that however keen she was to see Miss Rome, she couldn't let Sophie go back to Caldicott Place on her own. Yet it seemed idiotic to have got so far and not go on.

"Well, there's my ticket. You said you'd lend me the fare."

Whatever faults Sophie had she was not mean about money. She felt in her pocket and brought out her purse. She gave it to Carol.

"There's more than five pounds in there. That'll be heaps."

Carol could not see the purse but she could feel that it was full. Sophie's natural generosity made Carol more sure than ever that she should have been nicer to her. Now she not only wanted Sophie to come to London with her but she wanted, really wanted, to be kind to her. And so she found the right thing to say.

"Please come with me, Sophie. I'm scared to go alone. It won't be half as much fun without you."

Sophie gave a gasp and flung her arms around Carol's waist.

"Of course I'll come. Do you know that's the nicest thing anyone ever said to me."

10.
The Search

Mrs. Pennywell was the one who discovered that Carol and Sophie were missing. She had given Bill, Freddie, Athene and Tim their breakfast. Three times she had gone to the bottom of the stairs and beaten with a spoon on a saucepan, shouting:

"Carol! Carol! Sophie! Sophie! Come on down to your breakfasts."

After the third time she lost patience.

"I never met such lie-abeds," she said to the others. "No, Athene," for Athene was half out of her chair. "You finish your breakfast. I'll call those two and give them the edge of my tongue. Holidays it may be, but not down by after nine is going too far."

A few minutes later she clattered back, redder in the face than usual, panting and holding a hand over her heart.

"What's up?" Bill asked.

"They're not there. I don't believe Sophie slept in her bed. Lay on it, more like."

The other three looked at each other in horror.

"Oh, my goodness!" said Bill. "She's done a bunk. Mr. Crome senior said she might."

"But where's young Carol?" Mrs. Pennywell asked. "She wouldn't run away."

"Perhaps she heard Sophie and went after her," Athene suggested.

Mrs. Pennywell had got her second wind. She sat down in Carol's place at the table. Then she said:

"You boys go over to Winsford Halt and ask if Sophie caught the train. There's one a day from there, goes early picking up milk." She turned to Bill. "Carol knows better than to cadge a lift with strangers, doesn't she?"

"Of course," said Bill. "But if Sophie did I suppose Carol might go with her to look after her."

116

Mrs. Pennywell got up. "I'll telephone the police station."

"I'll give Jelly something belonging to them to smell," said Tim. "I bet he'll track them down."

"What about Mum?" Bill wondered. "I suppose I ought to telephone the hospital to tell her."

"Far better to telephone Jim Crome," said Athene. "He's such a comforting sort of man, he's sure to know what to do."

Bill agreed with her. "Right. I'll do that, but first the Halt. Come on, Freddie."

It proved much more difficult to get news at the Halt than the boys had expected. There would be no other train through the station until the evening when the milk train came back. So the station staff, whoever they were, went off duty.

"I expect they go to sleep," Freddie said. "That's what I'd do if I had to get up in the middle of the night to see a train out."

Near the Halt there were two cottages. Nobody seemed to be moving about in either. Bill nodded toward them.

"We'll have to try and wake somebody up. I bet whoever runs the station lives in one of them."

At the first cottage, knock as they would, they could get no reply, but at the second, after several knocks, an old woman came to the door.

"Does somebody who works at the station live here?" Bill asked.

"What?" said the old woman. "Speak up, I'm hard of hearing."

Bill raised his voice and repeated his question.

The old woman thought that over. "Would it be George you was wanting?"

"Does George work on the railway?" Bill roared.

"That's right. But he's sleeping now. He goes back to bed after the 2:30."

Freddie took a hand. It was unlikely he would make the old woman hear but he felt he must help.

"I'm afraid you'll have to wake him," he said.

Oddly enough the old woman heard Freddie's attempt at a shout.

"I daren't do that," she said. "Very nasty he can be if woke before ready."

Freddie could see Bill might lose his temper so he said quickly: "A little girl is missing—perhaps two girls. We must know if they were on the train."

Freddie, now that he was really trying, was producing a remarkably loud voice and it had a wonderful response. A window above their heads was flung open and a tousled red-headed man looked out. He sounded angry.

"What's all this? Can't a man enjoy his sleep without all this argy-bargy?"

Freddie, still afraid Bill might be cross, answered for him.

"I'm so sorry to disturb you but a little girl is missing from Caldicott Place—perhaps two girls. Did they go on the train this morning?"

"Let me think," said the man. "There was Mrs.

Binding from the shop and little Alfie. 'Course I was seeing to the milk churns but, now you ask, it seems to me there might have been two girls. What you want is Leslie—he sells the tickets.''

"Where do we find Leslie?" Bill asked.

"Ah! Not till tonight you don't. He went up to London on the train. He's got his old mother what he visits once a month.''

Bill was mad with frustration. Freddy again took over.

"You mean nobody can tell us until the train comes back tonight?''

The red-headed man nodded. "That's about the size of it. Now, if you don't mind, I'll get into my bed.''

At Caldicott Place they found only Athene. She was doing the housework.

"Mrs. Pennywell,'' she told them, "has gone to the police station, and Tim is trying to get Jelly on the scent, so I thought the best way I could help was to get the house tidy.''

The boys told her of their lack of success.

"I think,'' said Freddie to Bill, "you ought to ring the police station. I mean, they could find out if the girls arrived in London. Somebody must have taken their tickets up there.''

"I'll do that,'' Bill agreed. "But first I'm going to ring Jim. He'll know what to do.''

Jim sounded wonderfully calm.

"Bother that child!'' he said. "But don't flap, she's the most experienced runaway in the country. However,

I'll nip off to the railway station now and find out if Sophie arrived there this morning. What puzzles me is Carol. Surely, if she is with her, she'd telephone. Where's your mother? Let me have a word with her. Or is it a hospital day?"

"Worse than that!" Bill exclaimed. "It's the day Dad's coming home."

"You've told the police, of course, that the girls are missing."

"Of course," Bill said. "Mrs. Pennywell is at the police station now."

"There's nothing more you can do at your end then," said Jim. "Carry on with whatever you were planning to do. I bet we'll have found the girls before your mother gets home. But tell Mrs. Pennywell to keep within hearing of the telephone. I'll ring at once when I've got some news. If Carol is with Sophie I'm certain nobody need worry."

Bill told Freddie and Athene what Jim had said, adding, "So I suppose we'd better carry on with the riding and you, Athene, had better go to Edup and her marmalade."

"It feels awful going on as if nothing had happened," Athene moaned. "I shan't be able to attend to anything Edup says."

It was remarkable how the emergency had strengthened Freddie's voice. It was now almost as loud as Bill's.

"All the same, Jim's right. It won't help if Mrs. Johnstone finds us all about the place when she brings Mr. Johnstone home."

Mrs. Pennywell, coming in at the door, heard this. "Too right, Freddie. Nor it won't help worry-gutting. Now, you boys, go and cut up some logs. I'm going to cook a special lunch. What we all need is our strength kept up."

It was at that moment that Tim and Jelly came in. Tim held out a handkerchief with an S on one corner and said, "It's Sophie's. Jelly found it."

"Where?" Bill asked.

"On the road nearly opposite Winsford Halt."

Mrs. Pennywell usually grumbled at Jelly because of paw marks, but now she looked at him with respect.

"Well, I never! Clever Jelly! I was just saying we'd have a special lunch. Now that goes for you too."

Carol found herself in the humbling position of taking her orders from Sophie. There was nothing about unofficial traveling Sophie did not know. At Winsford Halt Carol nearly gave up going to London, for Mrs. Binding and Alfie suddenly appeared on the platform.

"Oh Sophie!" she gasped. "Look! I'd hoped Mum wouldn't know where we'd been because I'd told her I'd take you out today, but now Mrs. Binding will tell."

"Don't be silly," Sophie said. She dragged Carol to the end of the platform where it was dark. "She hasn't seen us and now she never will."

Carol did not feel safe until the train had chugged out of the station and then she had to admit Sophie had been right. Nobody had seen them get into the train, not even the red-headed man lifting milk churns into the luggage van.

"Let's take one seat each and go to sleep," Sophie said.

It was then Carol became aware of how hungry she was. She wished now she had eaten some of the biscuits in the tin she had opened.

"I wish we had something to eat," she said.

Sophie looked pityingly at Carol. "Of course we've got food. I never run away without any." She felt in her pockets for the key to her case, and while she was looking for it found she had lost her handkerchief.

"Bother!" she said. "It must have come out when I gave you my purse. It doesn't matter, I've some clean ones packed."

Sophie certainly was the most experienced runaway. In the case, besides clothes, there were apples, oranges, bananas and some chocolate.

"Where did you get all this?" Carol asked.

"Took it. I always take food that will do for running away. If I don't use it I put it back."

Carol thought it was stealing to take food from her mother's larder, but she could hardly say so when she was practically aching from hunger.

After their meal the two girls lay down on the seats and went to sleep. If it had not been for a lot of banging and shouting they might have been shunted, still asleep, into a siding. As it was Carol sat up with a jump and looked out of the window. She gave Sophie a shake.

"Come on. It's London! Everybody has left the station but us."

Because they had overslept there was no ticket collector at the station, but this did not worry Sophie. There was a gate open and through this she marched.

"Come on. You better get washed and tidy if you're going to see your dancing mistress. You look a mess. Then we'll have breakfast."

After breakfast they put Sophie's case in the station cloakroom. By this time Carol was feeling nervous. It was ages since she had seen Miss Rome. What would Miss Rome think when she turned up without saying she was coming? Would she ask questions? If she did how could she explain how desperate she had been feeling? Suppose Miss Rome never had thought she could be a professional? After all, it was only the other girls who had thought so.

"I think perhaps I better ring up Miss Rome and ask if she will see me," she said.

Sophie was disgusted. "You really are soppy, Carol Johnstone. You come all the way to London to see Miss Rome and then you ring up and ask if she'll see you. What'll you do if she says no?"

"I hadn't thought of that," Carol agreed. "She might be surprised if I just walked in."

"Let her be," said Sophie. "We'll take a bus."

Miss Rome was conducting a class when the girls arrived. The assistant named Peggy who opened the door when Carol pressed the buzzer was amazed to see her. She had taught Carol so she knew her well.

"Carol Johnstone! I thought you were in the country."

"I am. I've just come up for the day. I must see Miss Rome, Peggy. Do you think she'll see me?"

Peggy looked doubtful. "You know what holiday classes are."

"I wouldn't keep her long," Carol pleaded.

Sophie, who never pleaded for anything, was shocked at Carol's humble tone. In her opinion that way of talking got nobody anywhere.

"Just go to Miss Rome," she told Peggy, "and tell her Carol has come all the way from the country to see her."

Peggy noticed Sophie for the first time. She laughed. "Hullo! Where did you spring from?"

"I'm Miss Sophie Jones. I'm a paying guest at Caldicott Place," Sophie explained, "and I was running away but now I've decided to go home with Carol."

Peggy looked at her watch. "Go into Miss Rome's office, Carol, and take Sophie with you. I'll catch Miss Rome and tell her you"—her eyes twinkled as she looked at Sophie—"and Miss Sophie Jones are here."

Twenty minutes later Miss Rome came into her office. She was an imposing-looking woman. As a girl she had been expected to have a brilliant future as a dancer, but she had grown too tall and had sublimated her ambition by teaching others to dance.

"Carol, my dear," she said. "What's brought you up here?"

Sophie did not like being overlooked. "Me. I'm Miss Sophie Jones. I ran away and Carol came too because she wanted to see you."

Miss Rome knew how to handle girls like Sophie. "I think, Miss Sophie Jones, I'd let Carol explain."

It was difficult for Carol to explain everything with Sophie there because, after all, the visiting children were one of the reasons why her mother had not had time to arrange about her dancing classes. But Miss Rome was nobody's fool and quite capable of reading between the lines. She heard about Tim's inheriting Caldicott Place and that Mr. Crome senior's three wards were staying for the holidays. "You see, Caldicott Place costs a lot," Carol explained. Miss Rome heard about Carol's father, though not that he was coming back that day. Then Carol got to the difficult part.

"Because of everything I can't get Mum to fix a dancing class. She doesn't even know the name of one, nor do I. I think it will have to be in Eastbourne. Could you look one up? I know they're all in books."

Miss Rome nodded. "Of course I can. But what made you come here? Why not telephone?"

Carol flushed. "I didn't think of it. I was getting desperate."

Sophie felt Carol was making a poor show of explaining. Besides, Miss Rome seemed to have forgotten there was somebody else in the room. She got out of her chair and lolled against the big office chair in which Miss Rome was sitting.

"Carol thinks it's awfully important where she learns. She thinks if she learns properly she'll be good enough to dance in a ballet."

Carol was furious. "I never said that and I never thought it. What I said was I might be a professional some day. That means any sort of dancing, not just ballet—but you're too young to know that, Sophie."

Miss Rome put an arm around Sophie. "And where do you come from, Miss Sophie Jones?"

Sophie was charmed. At once the hard-luck-story whine was back in her voice. Off she went on the long story of the adoption which never happened.

Before Sophie could start on another, Miss Rome, looking almost amused, asked: "And now that you're on your own in the cold, cruel world, who looks after you?"

"Well, Mr. Crome senior—but mostly Jim, his grandson, does the arranging."

"They're Rawson, Pulson and Crome," Carol explained. "The solicitors who had the arranging of Tim inheriting Caldicott Place."

Miss Rome pulled the telephone toward her. "Before we discuss dancing classes or your future, Carol, we must let Mr. Jim Crome know where you are. There's probably a police search for you both by now."

Jim was out so Miss Rome talked to Mr. Crome senior. He was very grateful that she had telephoned to him.

"We had heard the girls were missing. My grandson has gone to the station to try to ascertain if they traveled on the milk train. I am indeed sorry for any inconvenience you may have been caused by my ward. As soon as my grandson returns I will send him to relieve you of both Sophie and the Johnstone girl."

Miss Rome was amused. The precise voice conjured up such a clear picture of Mr. Crome senior.

"Thank you. I have an outside appointment but I have an assistant who can function for me until I arrive so I will wait here until your grandson turns up."

Peggy was just starting a class so Miss Rome sent Carol to join it.

"I'm sure you can borrow some shoes. It's a pity not to have a lesson as long as you are here." Sophie showed signs of following Carol but Miss Rome stopped her. "You stay with me, Sophie. I don't allow visitors while classes are in progress. I was about to have a cup of coffee while I wait for Mr. Crome senior's grandson. You can join me."

Sophie thought Miss Rome wonderful. She had a gift for listening and so seemed to Sophie the best audience she had ever had. She could not sit on Miss Rome's knee or hold her hand because you can't while you are drinking coffee and eating biscuits, but otherwise everything was perfect. Sophie told Miss Rome all about her schools and why she had run away from them.

"I would have run away from the last one too, but Mr. Crome senior said: 'Sophie darling, of course you needn't go back to that school if you don't want to. Your being happy is all I care about.' "

"And now you are going back to Caldicott Place?" Miss Rome asked.

Sophie finished a mouthful of biscuit. "I think so but it depends on Carol. She surprised me very much last night. She treated me like her little sister, which she never had before. If she goes on doing that I'll stay."

"Very good of you," said Miss Rome. "Tell me, Sophie, except running away what do you most like doing?"

Sophie thought. "Talking—you know, telling people things like I'm telling you."

"Do you ever write stories? Had you thought you'd like to write books some day?"

Sophie knew the answer to that. "No, I'd hate that. I like doing things myself, not writing about them. I simply hate it when they make us write stories in my schools."

The studio bell rang. Miss Rome got up and put the coffee tray on a side table. "That will be Mr. Crome's grandson," she said.

Jim came breezing in. Much to Sophie's annoyance he paid no attention to her. All his attention was given to Miss Rome.

"I hear you have an appointment. Can I drive you to it?"

"That's very kind," said Miss Rome. "It's to the Classic." Sophie got up to come too but Miss Rome stopped her. "No, you stay here. I want to talk to Mr. Crome. There are some magazines on that table you can look at."

When they got outside Jim said: "What's the betting Sophie's gone by the time I get back?"

Miss Rome shook her head. "I think not. I'm used to temperamental children. They usually do what I tell them."

Miss Rome was right. When Jim got back to the

studio he found both Sophie and Carol waiting for him. Carol had an expression like a dog who expects a beating. Jim laughed.

"No need to look like that at me, Carol. You're not my ward, thank goodness. What you do is your family's affair."

"But I'm your affair, aren't I?" said Sophie. She climbed into the seat next to him. "Are you angry with me?"

"No, just bored. You run away so often. But I don't mind so much this time as I was coming down to Caldicott Place anyway. I've had a letter from Freddie asking if I could."

"Oh him!" said Sophie. "You'll be surprised when you see him. He almost talks like other people now, though he's still a bit soppy. My case is at the station."

Jim nodded. "Right. We'll pick it up and then set off for Caldicott Place."

"What about lunch?" Sophie asked. "They'll have finished long before we get there."

"You really deserve to starve," said Jim. "But, as it happens, I'm hungry too so we'll stop on the road at a place I know. I couldn't ask Mrs. Pennywell to keep lunch hot for us—the poor woman's had kittens over you two as it is."

"What time will we get there?" Carol asked in an anxious voice.

But Jim reassured her. "I've heard all the news from Bill. You'll be home long before your mother is expected."

On the way to the station Jim talked to Sophie about herself but from a different angle.

"At your various schools have you acted in plays?"

"At all of them. Mostly at each school I was a child angel in the Nativity play though once I was St. Joseph. Then I was the caterpillar in *Alice in Wonderland* and at another school the Red Queen. My biggest part was the bad queen in *Snow White*. I liked being her."

"Nice bit of type-casting," said Jim. He drove into the forecourt of the station. "Now give me your cloakroom ticket, and I'll collect your case."

Jim was returning with the case when he ran into Mrs. Binding and Alfie. Mrs. Binding looked doubtfully at Jim and then a smile of recognition spread over her face.

"You're the young gentleman who stayed at Caldicott Place when the family were moving in."

Jim tried to think who she was and suddenly it came to him. "Mrs. Binding at the shop! And this is your grandson Alfie."

Mrs. Binding shook her head at Alfie. "We come up on the milk train. It was a reward before school starts, but he's taken ever so queer."

"I'm sorry for that." Jim looked at Alfie. "What's up, old man?"

Mrs. Binding answered. "Can't get warm and doesn't fancy anything to eat and his ears ache. I was going to take him home, but there isn't a train back till the milk train goes tonight."

Jim gave Alfie a friendly push. "In for a penny in

for a pound," he said. "There's my station wagon over there with Carol and Sophie in it. I'll drive you home. You can sit with me, Mrs. Binding, and the girls can look after Alfie in the back. And if you feel sick, Alfie, tell the girls in plenty of time so I can let you out."

Alfie was not sick, in fact he seemed to cheer up on the first part of the journey, and he even agreed to eat lunch. But after lunch he and both girls went to sleep and knew nothing more until the car stopped with a jerk. They were outside Mrs. Binding's shop and Bill, Freddie and Tim had opened the doors and were leaning over them.

"Well, of all the idiots!" Bill said to Carol.

Tim spoke to Alfie. "I rode all by myself. Freddie had a leading rein but he didn't have to use it."

"I say," said Freddie, helping Mrs. Binding out, "I am glad you could come down, Jim."

"Alfie's been queer," said Mrs. Binding. "Give him a pull out, will you, Freddie dear? I want to get him to bed."

Freddie and Bill hauled Alfie out of the car. He did look pale and sort of puffy so they pushed him into the shop. Tim was already sitting beside Jim so Freddie and Bill joined the girls in the back.

"And who's lucky!" Bill whispered to Carol. "Mum telephoned she's bringing Dad in a taxi. They won't be here for an hour so she'll never know what you've been up to."

11.

Arrival at the Lodge

The lodge looked really nice, simple and friendly and welcoming. Proudly Mrs. Johnstone threw open the front door. There was a big log fire in the little sitting room and the table was laid for tea. It really did look cosy.

"Here you are, darling," she said to her husband. "This is your own house. Nobody will bother you here."

Mr. Johnstone looked around with a scared air.

"Thank you," he said and then, without looking at anything, sat down in the arm chair.

"The bedroom is up those stairs," his wife explained. "I'll go to the house now and see everything is all right, then I'll come back and have tea with you and unpack your things."

She might not have spoken for all the interest her husband took. He just sat gazing into space. Quietly she shut the front door.

Outside Caldicott Place she paused to get her face in order. She was sure that her unhappiness showed on it. She must look cheerful. The last thing she wanted was for the children to see how anxious she was. As it happened it was not the children she first saw but Jim.

"Jim! Am I glad to see you! What brings you here?"

"A variety of reasons. I needn't bother you with that now, Mrs. J. Why don't you go into the lounge and let me bring you some tea."

Mrs. Johnstone felt that she might easily cry; kindness is so hard to take when you are feeling low. She shook her head.

"I said I'd have it with him. Oh Jim, it looks so nice at the lodge but he wasn't a bit pleased."

Jim took her arm and led her toward the lounge.

"Come along, Mrs. J., and sit down. There's a splendid fire in here. I've seen to it myself. You expect too much. Give him a day or two to settle in."

"I know the doctor wants my husband to be on his own but I hate to leave him. After all, he's straight out of hospital and suppose he feels ill in the night?"

"Don't fuss about that," said Jim. "I was going to suggest asking Mrs. Pennywell to make up a bed on the sofa in here but instead why don't I sleep in the sitting room at the lodge?"

Mrs. Johnstone's face lit up. "Oh Jim, would you? I should be grateful. I can't sleep there myself because of the children."

Of course it took no time for the news to spread around the house that the children's mother was back. The children rushed into the lounge, Carol a little nervous; it would be so easy for someone to say the wrong thing.

"Mum! Mum!" said Tim. "I rode a pony all by myself."

"I didn't get on too badly, did I, Freddie?" Bill asked.

"Fine," Freddie agreed. "He takes to riding like a duck to water, Mrs. Johnstone."

Jim looked approvingly at Freddie. The holiday had done him good. It was nice to hear him speaking in an ordinary voice. Then he turned to Athene.

"And what has Miss Paxos been up to?"

"Making marmalade. Edup showed me how."

"When pressed?" Jim asked.

Athene laughed. "For once, no—for no pressing was needed. She's the champion orange-marmalade maker of something called the County Woman's Institute. She's won prizes."

"Why have you come?" Tim asked Jim. "There isn't a bedroom for you."

Jim rubbed Tim's hair up the wrong way. "You'd be surprised. I shall curl up under the dust sheets in one of those rooms you never use."

"Go and have your teas, darlings," Mrs. Johnstone said. "I'm a little tired so I'm having mine in here." Then she remembered the plans for Carol and Sophie.

"Did you and Sophie get to a film?" she asked Carol.

Carol gave Jim a desperate look. Jim saw it and that Sophie was preparing to answer, so he spoke before she had a chance.

"I met them on the road and drove them home."

"And he drove Mrs. Binding home too," Bill added. "Alfie's queer."

Jim felt that that was enough about the day's doings.

"Now do get a move on," he said. "Your Mum wants a cup of tea and a bit of hush."

Tim would not be hustled off. He had waited for what felt like hours to tell his mother about his riding lesson. He didn't believe she was too tired to hear about it. So when the other five ran down the passage in the direction of the dining room he loitered behind, half thinking of going back into the lounge. That was how he heard what Jim said.

"Sit where you are, Mrs. J. I'll bring your tea along, then I'll go straight across to the lodge and give the patient his."

Tim, followed by Jelly, ran so fast up the hall that he skidded.

"My goodness!" he whispered to Jelly. "Jim would think I was listening on purpose. But I wasn't—you know I wasn't. And do you know something else? Dad's at the lodge and they haven't told me. Why?"

When Tim had decided upon anything he saw what he wanted as clearly as if it was a lamp on a dark night. Ever since his father's accident what he had wanted was to see him again. For a time the wanting to see his father had been swamped in the need to find a home for Jelly. But now Jelly had a home—a super home—far better than anything he had ever known. That left only the other great want. He had watched with contentment the lodge being got ready. To Tim there was nothing strange in his father wanting to live in the lodge instead of in the house, for he would not mind living in the lodge himself. It would be like sleeping in his very own wigwam or in a tree house.

Every day as he had walked around the grounds he had noted things to show his father. "I say, Jelly, we must show Dad that when he comes." Or "Even though he's been ill I should think Dad could walk as far as this, wouldn't you, Jelly?"

For his father's arrival at the lodge Tim had something special planned. It was a secret which he had told nobody. It would please Dad even more than the gladioli he had never had. The grounds were what Mr. Crome senior had called neglected, but they had not always been. Among the tangled undergrowth garden plants still grew, including some rose trees; rose trees were some of the saved sights Tim had waiting for his father. The special surprise he had come upon quite by accident. He was prowling about getting to know every square inch just as Edup had told him he should, when he had fallen into a sort of hole. It was full of dead leaves, which he had scraped out, and there at the bottom were snowdrops. Bent and rather pale-looking but proper snowdrops such as were planted in the garden at home. Some even had flowers showing though their heads had not yet bent over as snowdrop heads do.

"Jelly," Tim had said, "look! Snowdrops. Dozens of them. When Dad comes we'll fill a vase for him. They'll make him feel better. I know they will."

And now Dad had come and there was no vase of snowdrops waiting for him. It would be impossible to find them in the dark. Should he wait for tomorrow and take them to Dad or should he just tell him about the snowdrops today? As he ate his tea he tried to make up his mind and by the time he had eaten his last mouthful he knew the answer. It was just the same as when Dad was in the hospital. Everybody—absolutely everybody—was trying to stop him from seeing Dad. They were all pretending he wasn't at the lodge. Well, he wasn't putting up with it. Directly tea was over he went upstairs and put on his gumboots and his thickest pullover.

"Quiet, Jelly," he said. "We want them to think I'm playing with my trains."

Jim had not stayed long with the children's father. He had not seemed to mind his being there, in fact Jim doubted whether he had taken in that he was there. He had sat quietly in the armchair while Jim made his tea in the little kitchen and put the tray beside him. Jim supposed that to Mr. Johnstone he was just like one of the orderlies at the hospital. So when he saw that Mr. Johnstone was drinking his tea he said:

"I'll leave you now. Someone will be across for the tray and to bring you your supper, and of course Mrs. Johnstone will see you into bed." He didn't add: "And then I'll sneak back and sleep by the fire."

Mr. Johnstone had looked at Jim as though he were seeing him through thick glass.

"Thank you. You are all very kind."

"Phew!" thought Jim as he walked back toward Caldicott Place. "I suppose the doctors know what they're talking about but I wouldn't let him out of the hospital myself."

Tim, holding Jelly by the collar, was hiding among the trees. He saw Jim come out of the lodge and he waited until he was safely out of hearing distance. Then he ran across a little path and opened the gate.

The wound had now completely healed on his father's head. Perhaps he was paler than he had been before the accident, but to Tim he was Dad as he had always known him. He was so pleased he had a lump in his throat so big it nearly choked him.

"Dad!" he gulped. "Dad!" and flung himself into his father's arms.

Jelly, feeling the excitement in the air, was not to be left out. With shrill barks he jumped up, trying to lick Tim's father's face.

There was a pause which Tim, still ecstatically mur-

muring "Dad! Dad!" didn't notice. Then, as if a shutter had opened in a closed house, his father's face lit up. Then he said:

"Jelly! Good old Jelly! Where have you been all this time?"

Tim did not risk staying long. To him the visit was entirely satisfactory. He did all the talking, which was to be expected because he had such a lot to tell. The things he had saved up for his father to see. The place he was to fish. About his riding lesson and, of course, the snowdrops.

"School starts again, worse luck," he said, "but on Saturdays and Sundays I'll help you make a garden. You'll hardly have to buy anything because mostly garden things grow wild here. When Mum comes don't tell her I've been here because she's fussy about you seeing people. It's because you've been ill, I suppose." He had given his father a hug. "Good night. Now that you're back everything is absolutely perfect. It nearly was before except for an awful girl called Sophie, but she goes away in four days."

Because he was expecting it Tim was not in the least surprised when his father said, "Good night, old man. Good night, Jelly." How was he to know that had the doctor heard him remember Jelly's name he would have danced a hornpipe? But nobody knew, for when an hour later the children's mother came to the lodge the patient, as far as she could see, was sitting just as she had left him and was still taking no interest in anything.

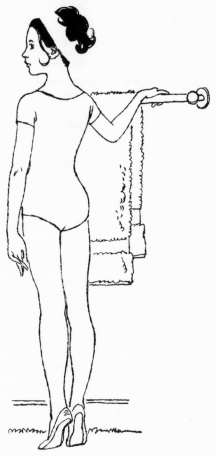

12.
Quarantine Holiday

Term for Freddie was four days away and for Athene three, but no arrangements had yet been made for Sophie.

"Isn't it odd," Freddie said at breakfast the next morning, "When the holidays start you think they're going on forever and ever, then suddenly it's almost time to pack."

Athene never spoke about her school, which was the most expensive girls' school in the country. But now she suddenly burst out:

"It's much worse for me than for you, Freddie, because I have to go first. Just think of me waving good-by while the lucky rest of you stay here."

"I doubt that happening," said Jim. "If you can bear it, Mrs. J., I thought I'd stay until Athene has to leave and then I'd take Freddie too. My grandfather can put you up for the night, Freddie."

"And what about me?" Sophie asked. "Where am I going?"

Jim had talked to Mrs. Johnstone the night before. Now seemed a good moment to break the news about what they had discussed.

"You're staying here, at least until half-term. You'll go to the same school as Tim."

There was a horrid silence. The Johnstones were all appalled. Tim thought it was going to be hard enough sneaking off to see his father, but it would be much worse with that awful, sharp-eyed Sophie, who always wanted to be with people, hanging about.

Bill almost groaned out loud. If somebody had to stay why did it have to be Sophie? What was Jim thinking about? There must be a boarding school somewhere which would take her.

Carol was the most dismayed of the lot. Miss Rome had not given her the name of a dancing school or said anything about her chances of being a professional after Sophie had blurted out that was what she wanted to be. But Peggy had been comforting. "Miss Rome will think of something. She's always been interested in you. You leave it to her." Carol had determined to make a real effort to be nicer to Sophie, partly because she had paid her fare but mostly because she had liked her better on the journey to London. But meaning to be nice to a person, even a sister to her, was one thing when you thought she was going away in three or four days. But half a term! However, it was terribly noticeable that nobody was looking pleased so she tried hard.

"That's good."

Jim gave her a funny look—half grateful, half amused.

"At half term I may have thought up something you'll like," he said, but it was at Carol he was looking, not at Sophie.

Jim was a great addition to the household. He was full of plans.

"I thought we'd go to Brighton today. We'll have lunch there."

"Oh Jim, how kind!" said Mrs. Johnstone. "It would be a help."

But there were protests as well.

"I wanted another riding lesson this afternoon," Bill said. "Freddie's ordered the ponies."

"We'll have an early lunch," Jim promised. "I'll get you back in heaps of time."

Freddie hated wasting one of the few mornings he had left away from Caldicott Place. There was so much he wanted to do—things like cutting a huge pile of logs, and putting a coat of paint on the garage. But he said nothing for he could see that taking them all out would make it easier for the patient at the lodge to be kept quiet.

Athene protested. She had only three days left and she was not going to waste one doing an everyday thing like eating in a restaurant. She had by degrees taken over certain jobs from Mrs. Pennywell and was not willing to part with one before she needed to.

"Do you mind, Jim, if I stay here? I help Mrs. Pennywell every morning and I love it."

"It's true," said Carol. "You won't believe it, nobody would, but Athene likes—really likes—doing housework."

Jim was going to say that Athene could stay but before he could speak Tim said:

"Jelly and me don't want to go to Brighton. Edup said I was to visit every square inch of my property to let it know I was pleased to know it, and that is what me and Jelly are going to do."

Jim was sorry for Athene but if he made an exception for her he must make one for Tim, and Tim roving about was the last thing anyone wanted the first morning after the patient arrived.

"Sorry, everybody, but you're all coming to Brighton. Mrs. Pennywell needs one day off from feeding you wolves."

In spite of those who didn't want to go the morning in Brighton turned out well. After a splendid lunch the party came home in plenty of time for Freddie to give Bill his riding lesson. He had offered to hire a pony and give Tim a second lesson too but Tim refused. It was gorgeous learning to ride but showing Dad where the rose trees grew would be even more gorgeous.

Arriving at the village, Jim stopped outside the shop.

"Your mother said we were to pick up some things here. Nip in, Bill, and get them."

But before Bill had time to open the car door Mrs. Binding had come out to them.

"Oh, I'm so glad to see you. The doctor's just gone. I had him because Alfie was all swollen up. I thought it might be a tooth but it wasn't. He's got mumps."

"Even if they don't go and catch the mumps," Mrs. Pennywell told Edup the next day, "which they most likely will for none of them has had it, just think what the house is going to be like! Six of them for another three weeks with no schooling."

"If pressed," said Edup, "I don't mind teaching the girls a bit of cooking. Teaching Athene will be a pleasure and I suppose young Carol can learn."

Mrs. Pennywell thought the idea a good one.

"You can't catch the mumps for you had it something terrible when you were a baby. The doctor said he never saw it worse."

"How they making out up there?" Edup asked.

Mrs. Pennywell laughed.

"Well, you can imagine that when they all come in shouting the news Mrs. Johnstone was knocked all of a heap. Well, I mean, who wouldn't be? Two of them expected to be off to their boarding schools and the rest to the day schools before a week's out, and then at a snap of the fingers, as you might say, all back on her hands. And, mind you, that on top of Mr. Johnstone being in the lodge."

"He's coming on nicely."

Mrs. Pennywell shook her head. "That's not what Mrs. Johnstone says."

Edup looked up from the brussels sprouts she was peeling. "I've no patience with him myself. I mean, living by himself in the lodge. It isn't natural. And he can talk at bit when he has the mind to. As you know, seeing I was pressed, I go in every day to clean up and see to the fire and that. At first it was all I could do to get a 'good morning' out of him. But now he says a few words about the weather and that. If he was mine I'd put on his coat and send him out, for I reckon a brisk walk is what he needs. Too much coddling never helped anybody."

"That's right," Mrs. Pennywell agreed.

Edup nodded. "I was saying to Sam, 'Even if you fall off a ladder on to your head don't think you'll get a cottage to yourself because you won't.' He didn't half laugh. When are the children coming to see their Dad?"

"Any time. I mean, Mrs. Johnstone doesn't want to make a thing of it. She was saying that she wanted them to drop in natural like. Carol could go in to pick up a tray and Bill to take him the newspaper, something of that sort. They're not telling Tim he's there yet."

145

"That's plain silly," said Edup. "There's no flies on young Tim. He'll find out for himself. You'll see."

Mrs. Pennywell was quite right when she said Mrs. Johnstone was knocked all of a heap when she heard about the mumps.

"Oh Jim!" she groaned. "I can't bear it. I know I'd agreed to keep Sophie for half a term to help you out. But she was to have been at school all day. I don't want my three about until their father's got used to being here, let alone your three. You don't know anywhere else yours could go, do you?"

"Have a heart, Mrs. J.," Jim said. "Where could I put three children who are in quarantine for mumps? But I tell you what I will do. I'll ask my grandfather to let me stay away from the office for three weeks. That'll mean you have the use of my car with me as chauffeur. I can at least take all six out to meals."

"Where?" asked Mrs. Johnstone. "You're forgetting they are in quarantine."

"Well, picnic lunches then," Jim suggested.

"In January!" Then Mrs. Johnstone smiled. "All the same it's a noble offer and if you can bear that makeshift bed at the lodge I'll be thankful to have you. The children can eat here; after all, as I'll be paid for keeping them I can still have Mrs. Pennywell. I had arranged to cut her down to two mornings a week after school started."

An unexpected holiday is something most children are pleased to have and Athene and Freddie were thrilled, but very conscious of the fact that they had been wished on to Mrs. Johnstone, so both tried extra hard to help. As neither Bill nor Carol really liked domestic chores, though this didn't cause a quarrel, it did cause a sort of uneasiness.

"All right," Bill would grumble to Freddie. "I don't mind digging up that bit of land where Mum wants a vegetable garden but don't go on about it. There's no rush. Anyway I should think she'll get Sam to do it and he'll be far better than us."

"There's no need to absolutely slave at housework," Carol would growl at Athene. "Of course we all want to help but there's no point in doing so much that Mrs. Pennywell has nothing to do."

The trouble was not so much that the guests were making the Johnstones look lazy as that Bill and Carol were worried sick over their father. They both dropped in each day and saw him casually but he frightened and shocked them. They talked about it together.

"He isn't like Dad at all," said Carol. "He just sits and when I kiss him it's not like kissing him, more like kissing something made of china, and he never hugs me back. He doesn't seem to know it's months that he's been away."

"I know," Bill agreed. "He's the same with me. I say, 'Hullo, Dad!' and he says 'Hullo, old man!' and that's that. It's so difficult to say things to him when he only half knows you are there."

"Whatever happens," said Carol, "let's keep Freddie and Athene from seeing him. They'll think he's dotty."

The word "dotty" lay between them. Both would have sworn their father was miles from being dotty but both dreaded the word.

"I'll tell Freddie and Athene to keep away," Bill offered. "They won't mind. What about Sophie?"

"I'll tell her something," said Carol. "She's still hanging around me, pretending we're sisters. It's a bit of a nuisance but if it stops her running away it's worth it, I suppose. Poor Mum, she's got enough with Dad at the lodge and us likely to have mumps."

Soon after the quarantine holiday had started Carol had heard from Miss Rome about a dancing school. She could not, of course, go there until she was out of quarantine but her mother rang up the school and explained and got Carol registered. Once she knew her dancing class was fixed, Carol unpacked her shoes and started daily simple practice, using the towel rail in the bathroom as a bar.

"Why don't you give Sophie some lessons?" Jim suggested. "You might find going back to the beginning useful, and it would certainly be nice for Sophie."

Carol thought teaching Sophie would be a bore but it wasn't. Sophie was so pleased that Carol wanted to teach her that she worked really hard and got on surprisingly well. She didn't show any special aptitude but she enjoyed learning.

Also, at Jim's suggestion, Bill taught Freddie some chemistry. Not ordinary school stinks but experimental chemistry.

"He's teaching you to ride," Jim said, "so why not

return the compliment by teaching him how to blow the house up."

Freddie found Bill's sort of chemistry fascinating. Jim would have had a fit if he had known how nearly his ward had come to blowing up Bill's bedroom with, of course, himself and Bill in it.

Tim, by careful watching, discovered the right times for himself and Jelly to visit his father. He also learned that some of his plans he had to give up. His father would not come to look at the spot where the rose trees grew, nor would he come to see the snowdrops. Nor could Tim pick a bunch as he had planned, for Mum would be sure to ask where they had come from. But these things didn't worry Tim. He remembered that after he himself had been ill with measles his legs had felt like cotton wool; no doubt, he thought, that's what has happened to Dad's. It was the same about plans. Dad was much slower at doing things than before he was ill, but again that did not worry Tim. He was sure he would be just as he had always been in the end.

"I think just outside the door would be an easy place for a garden to start with," he would say hopefully. "Would you like Sam to dig it up or could you and me do it?"

Often all his father would answer was, "A garden?" in a puzzled voice, as if he couldn't remember what a garden was. Then sometimes he would remember things clearly. Once he said: "Let's plant gladioli, Tim. I used to grow some lovely glads."

Then it was February. Quarantine was almost over.

It rained all the time but all the same there was a growing smell in the air. Mrs. Pennywell proved things could grow for she brought the children's mother a little vase of witch hazel. Jim was arranging to drive Freddie and Athene back to their schools, and he had told his grandfather he could expect him back at the office. Then two things happened. One everybody knew about but the other only Tim and Jelly knew about. In the middle of a dancing lesson Sophie burst into tears.

"I'm sorry, Carol," she sobbed, "but I can't do it, my ears hurt."

At the same time, down at the lodge his father had said to Tim:

"Could you get me a big garden fork? We might make a start on that digging."

The moment the children's mother knew for certain that Sophie had the mumps she made a prophecy.

"I'll tell you what's going to happen, Jim. The children are going to have the disease one after another. We'll be lucky if we're free of mumps by Easter. And it would be Sophie who got it first for when she's over it she can't be sent to school on her own. I'll still have her underfoot all day."

"Saying"—Jim imitated Sophie's whine—"what shall I do now? Nobody wants to play with me."

"Poor Sophie!" Mrs. Johnstone sighed. "I do hope she's been fairly happy here."

Jim looked like somebody with a secret.

"Don't worry too much about Sophie. I'm passing on

an idea to my grandfather, and if it works it'll be good news I hope for you too."

"Oh dear!" said Mrs. Johnstone. "Don't talk about your grandfather. I hate your having to go back to London. We shall all miss you terribly."

"Well, at least you're not going to miss the car," Jim promised. "Freddie had told me how badly a car was needed here, and it is. So he and I had a talk with Sam. Well, he's got some days off—he calls them lieu days— they are days which were public holidays on which, for some reason, he had to work. Well, Sam can drive and he has a friend from whom he can hire a car." He imitated Sam. " 'Not what you would call a smart job, sir, but reliable. It's black on account it mostly goes to funerals.' Anyway, you tell Mrs. Pennywell when you want the car, giving a day's notice if possible. She'll tell Edup, then Sam will bring it around and take you where you want to go."

There seemed no point in keeping the other children away from Sophie so, for the few days that she was in bed, her room became a dropping-in place for everybody. Sophie loved it.

"I have had a lovely time having mumps," she told Mrs. Pennywell. "Everyone's been so nice to me."

Mrs. Pennywell had come in with a jug of lemonade. Now she put it on the bed table and sat down beside Sophie.

"You're a funny one, you are. When you're well and having what most kiddies would call a good time it's whine, whine from morning to night. Now, when you can't open your mouth properly because of your glands being so swoll up, you are a different child. Never a grumble out of you."

Sophie tried to explain. "I wouldn't whine ever if people were always nice, but mostly they're horrid to me."

"No one's horrid to you so I've noticed. You get what you give in this world, don't forget that. Maybe you did have a bad start but no worse than many others, and you don't want to keep harping on it."

Sophie, ill or well, never admitted she was wrong so Mrs. Pennywell had no idea whether what she said had sunk in. Certainly while she was ill everyone praised Sophie.

"You can't help being fond of her when she's like this," Carol told her mother. "She's sort of cuddly."

Because Sophie was in bed and therefore get-at-able at any moment Mrs. Johnstone spent a lot of time with her. She brought whatever she was doing to the bedside, usually some mending.

"I ought to try to get you to school when you are better," she told her. "But you can't go alone and Sam can't drive you every day."

"I don't mind. I don't like schools anyhow. Do you know, Mrs. Johnstone, I feel sick when I wonder where they are sending me at half term."

Mrs. Johnstone remembered the look on Jim's face and what he had said.

"Jim may surprise you. He said he had an idea for you he was passing on to his grandfather. He said if his idea came off it would be good news for me too."

Sophie hugged her knees. "What sort of surprise, do you think? Could it be a governess here for me and Carol?"

Mrs. Johnstone saw in her mind's eye a smart, clever young woman who would have to be fed and looked after, and who would think her a fool and show it.

"No, Sophie. It can't be that. Jim knows me too well to think I'd think a governess living in the house good news."

"Would you like her if she was French?"

The children's mother had only the worst kind of school French so she shuddered.

"French would be worse."

"Well, it can't be sending me to a school abroad," said Sophie. "For Jim knows that now I call myself Carol's sister I don't want to leave her ever."

Sophie soon had a chance to prove how fond she was of Carol. For no sooner was she up than Carol caught mumps. She had it very badly with a high temperature. To start with nobody could use Carol's room as a dropping-in place for she was far too ill. And when she began to get better nobody wanted to drop in because she was so cross. Nobody, that is, except Sophie who from the beginning had insisted on being Carol's nurse.

"Let her," Mrs. Pennywell advised. "It makes Sophie feel wanted and is a help to us. I don't mind taking her up fruit juice and that but, with Sophie wanting to do it, why trouble? All she needs is a lamp and she'll turn into that Florence Nightingale."

Freddie and Bill most conveniently had mumps together. They were neither of them bad and managed to amuse each other. Then, just as they were recovering, Athene's glands began to swell.

The trouble with Athene's mumps was the trouble it caused. Of course as each of his wards got ill Mr. Crome senior was told. In the case of Sophie and Freddie there was no one to pass the news on to, but with Athene it was different. A cable was sent to her parents. It simply said, "Athene has mumps. Crome."

The next day Jim, giggling, was on the phone.

"You are to expect a specialist sometime today. The Paxos' cabled to us saying, 'Fly best specialist to Athene immediately. If necessary arrange for him to stay and kindly arrange for nurses.' "

Mrs. Johnstone repeated feebly: "Fly! Nurses!"

"They were thinking of a helicopter, I suppose, but it's simpler for the specialist to come by car. His name is Sir Bulwer Bone. We thought we had better choose a knight."

"Athene isn't at all bad," said Mrs. Johnstone. "She isn't even in bed."

"Put her there until old Bone has gone. I've tipped him off not to order nurses."

"No indeed! Nurses!" Mrs. Johnstone sounded quite faint. "What would we give them to do?"

Sir Bulwer Bone was very nice and not a bit pompous. He spoke to the local doctor on the telephone, and, after examining Athene, said he would tell what he called

"old Crome" to wire the Paxos' that there was no cause
for anxiety.

The next day presents began to arrive. First, a vast
crate of expensive fruit. Then an assortment of invalid
foods. And finally forty books.

Sir Bulwer had suggested that as her family were
anxious about her Athene should spend a day or two
in bed. As each crate or box arrived Mrs. Johnstone
apologetically brought up assortments from each.

"The things they come in are simply enormous. We
couldn't get them up the stairs so I've had to unpack
them in the hall. Just let me know when you want some
more and I'll bring them up. I'm afraid we'll have to
help eat your fruit. There are forty peaches as well as
masses of everything else."

Athene felt quite ashamed.

"Oh, do get everybody to eat it and give as much as
she'll take to Mrs. Pennywell, and send some to Mrs.
Binding and Alfie and to Edup and Sam, and of course
some to Mr. Johnstone. I'm terribly sorry about it all
but it's always like this. I can't have a cold without
Daddy and Mummy sending me a whole store full
of stuff."

Mrs. Johnstone looked lovingly at Athene. She had
become fond of her. It was incredible to her that
Athene's parents, who seemed to love her, could be happy
seeing so little of her.

"I have been wondering. Do you know where you
are going at Easter for we'd love to have you. In fact
we'd love to have you whenever you are free to come

to us. I mean, I could keep this room for you and call it yours."

For a moment it looked as if Athene were going to cry. Then a lovely smile lit her face.

"Oh, Mrs. Johnstone! You just can't think how happy that makes me. Having a place I can always come to. You did mean I could leave things in this room?"

"Of course. Anything you don't want at school. It's your room as long as we live here."

Athene flung her arms around Mrs. Johnstone's neck.

"Thank goodness you've had mumps so I can kiss you."

While all this mumps was going on Tim and his father were making a garden. Mrs. Johnstone—no gardener herself—supposed Sam was responsible and asked about it.

"I see someone has been digging. What a good idea! Is it Sam?"

Having been silent for so long Mr. Johnstone still found talking difficult so he didn't answer. It was going to cause such a lot of chatter and produce unwanted offers of help if he explained.

Freddie and Bill, before they had mumps, were busy with what was going to be a kitchen garden, so they too thought the digging in the lodge garden must have been done by Sam. But in their case they didn't ask.

Carol hardly saw any signs of digging before she went down with mumps. And she didn't ask about it because she had got into the way of saying as little as possible when she was with her father. So that Tim and his father sometimes worked for two hours on end and making a garden was known only to Edup. Edup thought digging was just what Mr. Johnstone ought to be doing, so she was careful never to mention what he was up to even to Sam for fear somebody stopped him. She also approved of the way Tim worked with his father. And in her way she showed him she approved.

"If there's to be a garden, plants and seeds and that will be needed. If pressed I could get them and nobody the wiser."

"I'm hoping," Tim explained, "that soon Dad will come around the place with me. There's lots growing that belongs to a garden. Yesterday I saw a primrose bud."

"That's as may be," said Edup. "But a new garden wants starting right. You and your Dad make a list of what's wanted and I'll see it comes."

So after his father had eaten his tea and someone had taken away and washed up the tea things Tim and Jelly would slip into the lodge and Tim and his father would pore over seed and plant catalogues and make lists. His father had no difficulty in talking then, but Tim didn't notice this particularly; after all he was expecting him to get well. Nor was he surprised, though tremendously pleased, when his father said one evening:

"I'd like to have a look at these grounds of yours tomorrow."

But when the next day came Tim woke up feeling most peculiar and when he felt his neck it was swollen on both sides.

"Mumps!" he told Jelly. "Mum is sure to say I've

got to stay in. It *would* be the very day Dad said he'd go for a walk." Then he sat up for he noticed a swishing noise. It was rain against the windows. Not ordinary gentle rain but a full-scale storm.

Tim got out of bed. He hung over the banisters and shouted as loudly as his swollen face would let him.

"Mum! Mum! I've got mumps." Then, with a pleased look at the rain-soaked window, he got back into bed.

13.
The Gathering Place

It rained for a whole week. Tim's mother was firm
with him.

"You're staying in until it's fine. Only an idiot would
want to go out in the rain when they've got mumps."

At the end of the week it suddenly stopped raining.

The sky turned blue with little fleecy clouds blowing across it. Primroses were coming out in every sheltered place. There were celandines growing on the banks of the stream. Among the primroses there were a few delicate whitish mauve flowers which Mrs. Pennywell called wind flowers but which Freddie said were wood anemones.

It was the end of the quarantine holiday. The children were all to go to school the next week. Jim was coming down the next day to fetch Freddie and Athene, and the others were to go by bus into Eastbourne. Tim had kept tabs on his father while he was ill. His first idea had been that Jelly would take notes. After all, a dog who could trace missing people ought to find taking a note easy. But Jelly detested rain, and the only exercise he agreed to take while Tim had mumps was when he was dragged out on the end of a lead. So Tim asked for help from Edup.

On his first day of mumps, he asked Mrs. Pennywell in what he hoped was a casual voice:

"Would you be seeing Edup today?"

Mrs. Pennywell was not fooled. "Out with it, young Tim. What you want Edup for?"

Tim had an answer ready. "She's getting me something for planting."

From the beginning there had been friendship between Edup and Tim and of course Mrs. Pennywell knew this, and knew what Edup had said about Tim getting to know his land. No doubt she and Sam had some stuff in their garden they didn't want and had

promised Tim he could plant it. Anyway it was important to keep him happy; his mother didn't want him
running around getting into draughts until his face went
down.

"You be quiet and look at that book," she said, "and
after dinner I'll slip along and see Edup. I have to go
to the shop anyway. If pressed I'm sure she'll pop up
and see you."

Edup had come the next day. Rain meant nothing
to her. In fact, when dressed in her big gumboots and
mackintosh, she rather liked it.

"Hullo, young Tim!" she said. "I just slipped in to
say your Dad's O.K. I told him you had the mumps and
he said quite natural like, 'Poor old Tim. Tell him as
soon as he's fit we'll go and see his land.' Then he takes
out the catalogues and that. 'May as well get this list
finished,' he says, 'for when this rain's over is just the
time to get planting.' Then, Tim, you'll never guess
what I heard next."

"What?" Tim asked.

"Upstairs I was doing the bedroom. Well, I couldn't
believe it, not right away, I had to come to the top of
the stairs to be sure I was hearing right. Your Dad was
whistling."

Tim tried to smile though his face was a bit stiff for it.

"Thank you, Edup, for telling me that. I'd forgotten
about whistling but before his accident Dad was a very
whistling sort of man. I expect his having started to
whistle again means he's almost well."

"Shouldn't wonder," said Edup. "Shouldn't wonder

neither if I made you one of my red current jellies. Slip down easy they do."

On that lovely day when the rain stopped, Tim, well-wrapped up and wearing his gumboots, was allowed to go out with Jelly. To Tim every step toward the lodge was magic. It was impossible to believe so much had happened in one week. He saw primroses and celandines. He found on some brushwood the beginnings of tiny leaves. He found the air was full of cheepings and chirpings.

"Absolutely dozens of birds must have moved in here while I've had mumps," he told Jelly.

Outside the lodge in a dark corner, which Tim had thought of as waste land, he had his biggest surprise. Sticking out all over it were green shoots with a pinkish shade around the stalks. He knelt down to examine them. The shoots, he discovered, were made up of neatly folded leaves.

"So you've found them for yourself."

Tim looked up. There was his father, dressed for gardening and carrying the fork Edup had got for him.

"What are they going to be?" Tim asked.

"Something you and I couldn't have grown in a hurry. These are lilies of the valley. Have to be settled, they do."

There was a lot of planting to be done, but it was such a lovely morning it seemed the right day for that first walk. With nothing said, Tim's father propped the fork against the house and the two of them crossed the path and made for the place where there had been a rose garden. His father was very knowledgeable and showed Tim lots of things he had missed.

"That green stuff is called dog's mercury and that is going to be a cuckoo flower. You're going to have bluebells in this wood, Tim."

Presently they sat on a tree that had fallen down, and Tim told his father what he could remember of what he had been told about Caldicott Place.

"We must find out about it, Tim," his father said. "I reckon that when your Lady Paine was a little girl there was a proper garden up by the house. There could be a plan somewhere. We might bring the gardens back."

Tim then had to ask a question which was bothering him.

"But when you're quite well we'll go home, won't we? When I told Mr. Crome senior I'd live here it was so you could fish—the doctor said you'd like to do that. And it was for Jelly—he was miserable without us and I was miserable without him."

Tim's father looked around him.

"This is a beautiful old place. The sort of place I've heard about but never seen. It's a shame to break it up." Then he looked at Tim as if he badly wanted somebody to understand. "It's queer, Tim, after the accident I felt sort of numb all over. You know, how your fingers feel on a cold morning."

Tim nodded. "And then they hurt when they get warm again."

"That's it exactly. Well, I've been getting warm again but it hurts. I suppose I've been playing a sort of game with everybody. Do you know, you and Edup are the only ones who know how much better I am."

"Mum must."

"She doesn't. Every day I've tried to tell her but I've felt sort of awkward. Can you imagine that?"

Tim couldn't. "Well, I'd tell her now. Freddie and Athene are going away this week and so there'll be more room. Why don't you come and live with us?"

For a second his father looked scared, then he took a grip on himself.

"I'm not quite ready for that, I'm afraid. But it'll come. Do you know where your mother is now?"

"She was going to the village but I expect she's back."

It clearly was hard to say but his father managed it.

"Fetch her, Tim. Fetch her now."

Tim found his mother tidying the lounge for Jim's arrival the next day.

"Oh Tim, have you wiped Jelly's feet?" she said, and then: "Go and get yourself a glass of milk."

Tim felt like anyone does who is going to give someone a lovely surprise.

"Dad wants me to bring you where he is."

His mother looked puzzled. "What do you mean, darling? You don't know, but Dad's at the lodge."

"I do know and he isn't. He's sitting on a tree in the middle of the wood waiting for you."

Tim had never been able to understand grownups. Most of the time they were sensible and ordinary and then suddenly they behaved as if they had gone mad. His mother behaved like that then. She caught hold of

Tim and nearly shook him.

"Say that again. Say it again."

"He's sitting on a tree in the middle of the wood waiting for you."

That seemed to make his mother queerer than ever. Instead of being pleased she burst into tears.

Tim gave Jelly a look which said as clearly as if he had spoken the word, "Women!"

Jim came down the next day. He thought he was the bringer of news but what he found was news waiting for him.

He heard it first from Bill and Freddie, whom he nearly ran over in the driveway. They stood on the running board on each side and shouted it at him.

"Dad's walking about."

"Mr. Johnstone has been to the wood."

"He's not coming to the house yet but Mum thinks he soon will."

As Jim stopped the car he said to Freddie:

"I don't want you back at the muttering stage but you've so much voice now you've nearly broken my eardrum."

"Do you suppose," Bill asked, "we'll be going home? I mean I suppose we'll have to when Dad goes back to work, won't we?"

Jim opened the door to let Lady out of the car. "What's the owner say?"

Bill laughed. "You know Tim. He takes everything as it comes. He doesn't seem a bit surprised that Dad went for a walk with him."

At that moment Tim, covered with mud and bits of dead leaf, came up to the house with Jelly at his heels.

"Oh good, Jim!" he said. "You've brought Lady. Jelly missed her last time."

Jim patted Lady.

"I could hardly bring her last time. I hardly brought myself, if you remember. I brought the girls, Mrs. Binding, Alfie and mumps. That was enough to be getting on with. I came without luggage and had to buy pajamas and a toothbrush."

In the hall Jim ran into Athene. "My dear Miss Paxos, I'm so sorry to hear you have had ear ache since the mumps."

Athene turned pink. "I didn't exactly write I had ear ache."

"Whatever you wrote to your parents, before you go back to school you have to see an ear, nose and throat specialist."

Athene looked miserably at Jim. "I just thought I'd like to get Easter settled. I know I can't go to Daddy and Mummy, but they might fly me out to relations in Greece and I'd much, much rather come here."

"I suppose, too, you remembered that flying wasn't good for sore ears?"

Athene nodded. "I did think that."

Jim laughed. "Well, you must tell the specialist what you were up to. Maybe he'll agree with you. Where's Mrs. Johnstone?"

Mrs. Johnstone was in the kitchen helping Mrs. Pennywell get lunch ready.

"Hullo, Jim dear! Have you heard the news?"

"Have I not! I'm hoping for an invitation to fish with him."

Mrs. Johnstone led the way into the lounge.

"It's wonderful! He's not back to normal, of course, but he's miles better. I mean, he's beginning to be interested in what goes on."

"Does he talk at all about going back to work?"

Mrs. Johnstone sat down.

"I'm not sure he'll do that. The doctor told me that something less hard would be better for him. We're turning over ideas. He's really excited about this place. Anyway it's too early yet for him to think about working at anything. Whatever he does his doctor won't allow him to go all-out for months."

Jim sat down facing her.

"Now listen to my news. You know a Miss Rome?"

"Yes, she taught Carol dancing. Why?"

"She has a niece who lives in Buckinghamshire who has a stage school." Jim was finding it difficult to explain as he had to leave out how he had met Miss Rome. "It's been suggested that sort of school might be just the place for Sophie. She's always dramatized herself, so perhaps a school of acting is what she wants."

"Good gracious!" said Mrs. Johnstone. "I should never have thought of that. Poor Sophie, she won't like leaving Carol for any school. I can't think why but suddenly she's become devoted to her. Treats her like an adored elder sister."

"If you agree, she hasn't got to leave Carol. There's

more than enough money to pay for both girls. At the stage school they teach dancing. My grandfather says that if you ask that Miss Rome, who taught Carol, she'll tell you the school would be just the place for her."

Mrs. Johnstone looked at Jim.

"You must think me a fool. How do you and your grandfather know Miss Rome? Come on, tell me the whole story. What have you been up to?"

The lodge became a gathering place for the household. Slowly, so slowly that nobody noticed, Mr. Johnstone began to take back his old place as the linchpin of his family. It was nothing that he did himself, it was just that, because he was there and interested, everybody discussed things with him.

As the only daughter, Carol had always been particularly close to her father. So now that he was back again it was to him she turned when she first heard of Jim's suggestion about Miss Rome's niece's stage school.

"In the ordinary way I'd have loved it, Dad, especially as Miss Rome says the dancing training is good, but I can't see me tagging along as a sort of relation of somebody's, can you?"

Her father was pricking out some snapdragon seedlings. He straightened up to look at Carol.

"We've heard from the insurance company; they are offering quite a large sum for the accident. I daresay I could manage the fees out of that. I mean, if you're going to have a career as a dancer it will be an investment."

Carol frowned, trying to find the right words.

"It's not Sophie paying so much as Sophie herself. I mean I didn't mind the three visitors coming for Christmas, we needed the money. But I didn't want them forever and ever. Now Freddie's got his room and Athene's got hers, and if I go to school with Sophie she'll be sort of part of the family. I mean we'll still have her when we eventually go home. Well, I wouldn't want that. Anyway there isn't a room for her and I'd hate to share."

Her father turned to gaze across at the wood. Though the trees were still mostly bare he knew where the catkins hung over the stream, and where the pussy willow was already haloed with its fuzz of yellow.

"This is a beautiful place, Carol. While we are here it's good that we can share it."

Carol turned and looked where her father was looking.

"It's pretty, but I don't like the country. I like towns."

Her father didn't seem to have heard what she said.

"She's a funny one, that young Sophie. If she can turn all that tale-spinning into acting there's no saying how she might turn out."

Carol was surprised. "I didn't know she'd been to talk to you."

Her father laughed.

"I don't think she's one to miss an audience. Sat on my knee and talked the hind leg off a horse. But there's truth behind what she says. She's had a bad start. She's very fond of you, Carol."

"Well, in a way I quite like her. She can be sort of cuddly, almost like a little sister. But do we want her for always?"

Her father turned back to his seedlings.

"I don't think you should let Sophie influence you one way or the other. The question is would you like to go to a theatrical school as a boarder? Do you want a career as a dancer? If the answer is 'yes' then leave it to me and your mother to arrange."

Put like that, Carol suddenly saw the theatrical school. A prospectus had been sent. There was a lovely photograph of a ballet class held in a long hall. There was a real little theater. The school, it said, trained boys and girls in all types of dancing as well as ballet, and they were taught to act. There were public performances each term. It sounded perfect. Imagine a world where everybody was interested in the same sort of things you were! And Dad was right, Sophie needn't spoil it. The prospectus said the juniors slept in dormitories but the middle and senior school shared three to a bedroom. She would be in the middle school. Oh, it was going to be heavenly! She flung her arms around her father.

"Please, Dad, I want to go. I want to go awfully. And I'll be nice to Sophie, truly I will."

Now that Mr. Johnstone was on the mend Mrs. Pennywell sometimes called in on her way home to see him. She thought it all wrong for a man to be living in the lodge when he had a wife and children up at the house. So she did what she could to speed his recovery.

"Young Tim says that you've never fished. Well, you want to get Sam of a weekend to teach you. Lovely trout there are in the stream."

"Is Sam an authority on fishing?"

Mrs. Pennywell roared with laughter.

"Not just fishing but your fish in particular. You see, when the place was lying empty, it was everybody's water like. Well, you couldn't blame them, could you?"

"I'll have to get a rod and a license, and you must give me a list of those who enjoyed fishing here."

"Sam will see to you. Come to that, I've a rod doing nothing you could buy. Pennywell, before he was took —food poisoning it was, a pie he ate on an outing—well, he was a great fisherman. I've got his basket, waders— the lot."

On another day Mrs. Pennywell did a little plain speaking.

"I'm glad you're getting on so well, because the children need you. Well, it's only natural, isn't it? A mother can't be a father and that's a fact. Bill's a grand boy but he needs you—easy to fool his mother—he's too busy with homework to give the help he might. Of course Tim is a different boy now that you're more yourself. Missed you cruel, young Tim did. I hear you've plans for Carol. I'm glad of that. Had a chip on her shoulder, she had."

"What about the visiting children? Did you like them?"

Mrs. Pennywell smiled.

"Leaving out Sophie—well, she's a card, that one— nicer young ones than Freddie and Athene you couldn't find. Seems funny to say so but I'm sorry for that Athene. She's got everything and nothing, you might say. All that money and those houses and those servants and all she wants is a proper home where she can help about the house. If I could meet her Dad and Mum I'd tell them something."

"And Freddie?"

"Oh, he's fine now. When he came he couldn't say boo to a goose and only picked at his food. But you can't carry on that way with our lot. A week with Bill and he was a changed boy; mind you, he did Bill a bit of good, come to that."

"Do you think Sophie's happy here?"

Mrs. Pennywell hesitated.

"We never told Mrs. Johnstone on account she was worriting about you, but she upped and run off one night."

The children's father laughed.

"So we heard. Mr. Crome told my wife about it. But I think she's settled down now, hasn't she?"

Mrs. Pennywell looked doubtful.

"I don't think young Sophie's the settling kind. One rough word and off she'd go."

It was Tim who told his father about the land, or rather what Mrs. Pennywell said about it.

"I know Lady Paine said I could sell Caldicott Place if I didn't want to live here. But Mrs. Pennywell says that everybody is proper scared it will be sold as a building site. She says they don't want none of that here because they're farming folk. When we go home must it be sold as a building site? Couldn't somebody else live here instead of us, Dad?"

His father was honest with him.

"I've been living out of things so long, Tim, that I've a lot of thinking to make up. But I promise you Caldicott Place is one of the subjects I shall give most time to thinking about. Give me a little longer and we'll talk again."

It was the week before Easter. Athene, who had got around the ear, nose and throat man, and Freddie were what they called "coming home" on the Thursday. Jim was bringing them down and staying over the weekend.

"Expect me plus Lady and fishing rods," he had written.

On Wednesday the family and Sophie were having a late breakfast. Suddenly the door of the dining room opened and Mr. Johnstone walked in.

"Dad!" Bill, Carol and Tim shouted.

"Hullo, Mr. Johnstone!" said Sophie.

Mrs. Johnstone was so pleased she couldn't say anything at all.

Her husband pulled up a chair.

"I'll have a cup of that tea," he said. "I've come home for good. When Jim comes he can sleep in the lodge. I've got schemes for Easter. If ever there was a place for an egg hunt this is it."

It was their father saying that that made the Johnstone children know he was truly well.

"Goody, goody!" said Tim. "Can I help?"

His father shook his head.

"You know you can't. I always like doing these things on my own. But I've some more to tell you. How would you like to live here always? I know what you feel, Tim, but how would you feel, Bill, and you, Carol?"

Bill was puzzled. "How could we? I mean when you go back to work."

"There's work and work. There's a lot to do to this place—to make it pay, I mean. You see, there are other children besides Freddie, Athene and Sophie who need a home in the holidays. With the compensation and what I'll get for selling the house, which the Robinson's want to buy, I reckon we could get by. But none of that answers my question."

Bill tried to think what he did feel. He had taken it for granted they were going home, probably in the autumn. Would he mind if they never went? Then suddenly he knew in a surge of happiness that he would be glad. Who would swap Caldicott Place for a small house in suburbia? He liked his new school. He liked Freddie coming for the holidays.

"I'd like to stay here."

"Good," said his father. "Now Carol."

Carol could see it was going to be one against four.

"I don't mind saying I'd much rather go home. I hate the country. But honestly, as I'm going to be a boarder next term, it won't matter much to me where I live. I mean, home is where you all are though I wouldn't say that if I had to be here all the time."

"Good," said her father. "That settles that. Your mother and I have already discussed it."

Sophie's chin shot up in the air.

"Does nobody care what Miss Sophie Jones thinks?"

Mr. Johnstone laughed.

"I'm coming to you. I've been having a lot of correspondence with Mr. Crome senior. If you're going to live with us we think we may as well make it legal. How would you like us to adopt you? You can be Miss Sophie Johnstone."

"My goodness!" thought Bill. "Dad is himself again. Imagine giving us an extra sister without asking us if we mind! And Sophie of all people."

Sophie did not jump at the suggestion. Instead she put on an aggravating, considering face.

Carol was furious.

"You really are the most extraordinary girl, Sophie. First you slop around everybody moaning that you've no family. Then Dad offers to join you to our family and you look at him as if he was only saying, 'Would you like some jam?' "

"You don't understand, Carol," Sophie whined. "As Miss Sophie Jones at least I'm me. A person on my own who can do things I couldn't do as the youngest Johnstone."

"What sort of things?" Tim asked. "Do you mean running away?"

"That for one," Sophie agreed.

Mr. Johnstone was starting with Sophie as he meant to go on.

"Take it or leave it. If we adopt you—and it's a big if, mind you—it'll be done legally through an adoption society. But that takes time. Any trouble with you during the waiting period and the offer's off."

Sophie pouted.

"I don't like people talking to me in that way." Then she got off her chair and climbed onto Mr. Johnstone's knee. "Actually, I'm saying 'yes' because I'm certain you'll get very fond of me."

"What about Freddie?" Bill asked. "Are you going to suggest adopting him?"

"No," said his father. "As you know, Freddie has a father living and special commitments, but he's to treat this house as his home and your mother and I will treat him as a son."

"From the sound of things," said Carol, "one day the Johnstones will be more like a clan than a family. I mean, if you're going to adopt all the children who've nowhere to go in the holidays."

"There are worse things than being a clan," said her father. "I'd like to see every bit of this house in use and that's a fact. It wasn't meant to be wasted."

It was a glorious Easter. Daffodils had sprung up all over the place. The banks were yellow with primroses. There was a fuzz of green on every tree. Everywhere birds were building their nests. Mr. Johnstone's egg hunt was up to his old form. He had bought dozens of eggs and hidden them in the most ingenious places. It took all day before they had found the lot, and there were not just the household looking but all the children from the village, led by Alfie. The grounds rang with shouts of, "I've found another."

Mrs. Pennywell, coming out for a breath of air,

watched Bill and Freddie lift Sophie so that she could take some eggs she had spotted out of an artificial nest. She watched Tim and Alfie scuffle for a group of yellow-wrapped eggs hidden in a clump of daffodils. With a smile she saw Athene clearing up the bits of paper dropped by the other children. Carol was not there for she was taking advantage of having the bathroom to herself to get in a bit of extra dancing practice holding on the towel-rail.

"Who'd think," Mrs. Pennywell said to Mrs. Johnstone, "it was only Christmas when you said to me: 'I'm not used to a place like this. I'm terrified of taking it on?' And now look at you all. You might have been here always."

Tim came panting up, his mouth all over chocolate.

"I shouldn't think there's ever been anybody happier than me," he said. "I do wish Lady Paine could see us."

"And who's to say she can't," said Mrs. Pennywell.